Samantha on Stage

Samantha on Stage

by *Susan Clement Farrar*

PICTURES BY RUTH SANDERSON

 *The Dial Press / New York*

Published by
The Dial Press
1 Dag Hammarskjold Plaza
New York, New York 10017

Copyright © 1979 by Susan Clement Farrar
Pictures copyright © 1979 by Ruth Sanderson
All rights reserved / First Printing
Printed in the United States of America
Design by Denise Cronin Neary

Library of Congress Cataloging in Publication Data
Farrar, Susan Clement. Samantha on stage.

Summary: Eleven-year-old Samantha had always been
the best in her ballet class, but when she saw
the new Russian girl dance she began to wonder who
would get the coveted lead in the school's
production of the Nutcracker ballet.

[1. Ballet dancing—Fiction. 2. Friendship—Fiction]
I. Sanderson, Ruth. II. Title.
PZ7. F2434Sam [Fic] 78-64958
ISBN 0-8037-7574-1
ISBN 0-8037-7577-6 lib. bdg.

To all my dear students
past and present who were the inspiration
for this novel

I would like to acknowledge my gratitude to the following people for their constant encouragement: Emily Saunders, Howard James, David Thompson, Elizabeth Woronzoff, Sally Clay, and of course my family.

Contents

Samantha on Stage

1

New Girl in Class

"Class, this is Lizinka Petrovna." Lizinka stood tall and straight, wearing a black leotard, her long, slim legs clad in pink tights and her feet in pink ballet slippers. Her dark-brown hair, braided and coiled halo fashion around her head, made her look every inch a ballerina. She nodded gravely to the class and, turning to Miss Jan, the ballet teacher, swept into a deep *révérence*, then quietly walked over to the ballet *barre* and joined the class.

"Lizinka has come here from Russia. Her father is a delegate at the United Nations. She has been studying ballet at the Bolshoi Academy for Children in Moscow, Russia. Let's all make her feel welcome."

As the class applauded lightly, there were a few giggles. Samantha, who was standing in front of Lizinka, turned and smiled, only to find Lizinka looking straight ahead, her left hand on the *barre* and her right arm rounded in second position, ready for her *pliés*. Her no-nonsense attitude took Samantha quite off guard, so that when the ballet teacher said, *"Pré-pa-ra-tion,"* Samantha was not ready for her *port de bras* and completely missed her first *plié*.

As they went through their *barre* work, Samantha, whom everyone called Sam, found it difficult to concentrate. She felt Lizinka's eyes boring into her back, and she knew that her own long, blond hair was unkempt compared to the properly upswept hair of the newcomer. Her face flushed with annoyance at herself, recalling Miss Jan's constant reminder: "A ballerina wears her hair up, making a more professional and neater appearance when doing *piqué* turns and steps of elevation. Besides," Miss Jan would continue, "the line of the neck is one of the most beautiful parts of the body and shouldn't be hidden."

"Why, oh why, didn't I take time to put my hair up?" Sam thought. She usually carried elastic bands in her ballet bag for that very purpose, but today she just hadn't bothered.

There were eleven girls in her ballet class. They

were all ten or eleven years old, and this was the year they were to go *en pointe*. The class had been together ever since the girls had started lessons at age six. For the past two years they had been working very seriously at the *barre*. This meant that they had to spend half an hour doing *grands pliés, tendus, battements, développés*. Bending and stretching— stretching and bending! Sometimes she wished they could forget it all and just *dance* — as when they did their center work and put steps together, or when they did their *diagonales* across the floor. . . . That was the part Sam liked best. *Piqué* turns, *élancés, tours jetés*—whirling and twirling and leaping, that was really fun.

But Miss Jan kept saying, "You are only as good as the *barre* work you do. Without it you can never improve. "Unless your body placement is perfect, your legs and back strong, I will not allow you to go *en pointe*," she would say. So they had no choice but to do the *barre* work.

Now, as the girls' muscles tingled and quivered, Miss Jan said, "Ready for the center work, class."

Twelve girls all rushed to the front line, laughing and shoving playfully. Samantha for some reason did not join the others, but stayed in the back line. Perhaps it was her unconscious desire to watch the newcomer, Lizinka. She was not going to have *her* eyes boring into her back again!

This was the part of the dancing lesson Sam loved!

She looked forward to the classical music playing softly as they all did their *ports de bras, balancés, jetés,* and finally, as a reward for good, attentive work, *piqué* turns diagonally across the floor. The class would get into a line at the far right-hand corner of the studio, and with the music playing quite fast ("allegro," Miss Jan called it), each did *piqués* to the left front corner of the studio. It was like a little solo dance with everyone watching.

Samantha felt a tingle of pride because she knew she could do them well. There was so much to remember! Not only did the footwork have to be just so, but each part of the body had a special task to do. The head must spin as she spotted. In order to do this the dancer must focus her eyes on *one* object. The arms must whip into middle fifth position, the body had to be straight and sure, with the shoulders pressed down and relaxed. She was the only one in the class who could do every part right. Even Miss Jan had commented on how beautifully she did her *piqué* turns. So it was with anticipation that she lined up ahead of Lizinka, confident of her ability in this area. She placed her foot in a lovely high *tendu,* and executing a *port de bras* as a *préparation,* she twirled across the floor in time to the beautiful music, her heart beating fast with joy. She stopped in a perfect fifth position, and as she turned to do her ballet walk back to the end of the line, a light round of applause from her classmates greeted her. She glanced over at the new girl to see her reaction, but Lizinka was staring straight ahead with no expression whatsoever that Sam could interpret.

And then it was Lizinka's turn. What was she doing? Her *préparation* was much more elaborate! Her *piqués*! She was twice as fast as Samantha. Even Miss Jan was so surprised and delighted that she started the applause herself!

Then it was time for the *grande révérence*. Each girl put one pointed toe forward, lifted her arms gracefully, and bowed formally to her teacher. The lesson was over for another week.

Chattering and giggling, the girls piled into the dressing room. Samantha followed quietly. Just as she turned to close the dressing-room door, she heard Miss Jan say, "May I see you for a moment, Lizinka?"

The phone was ringing when Samantha came in the door after her lesson. She ran to answer it, knowing that this was the afternoon her mother had to pick up her father at the train station.

"Hello?" Sam said breathlessly.

"Hi, it's me. Naomi," a cheery voice answered. "What do you think of *her*?"

"Of who?" Sam asked, puzzled, and then, "Oh, you mean the new Russian girl in our class. I don't know—she's a good dancer." Sam admitted this a bit reluctantly, frowning as she remembered Lizinka's double *tours*. Samantha had always been the star of her class. Dance came so easily to her that without half trying she had always excelled. Now here was a stranger coming into her class and outshining her.

"Wasn't it funny when she came on the floor and bowed to Miss Jan? I thought I'd die!" Naomi bubbled with excitement.

"I know it!" agreed Samantha. "She stood behind me at the *barre*, and I felt like such a klutz. I forgot my elastic bands again, and my hair was hanging down my back. Then when I did my *piqué* turns, it kept getting in my eyes—wow, was I ever mad at myself! I hope next week I remember. Uh-oh. Better go now, Naomi—my mom and dad are coming in the drive, and I promised to set the table. See you!" Slamming down the receiver, she ran into the kitchen and started rattling the dishes. She appeared to be very busy when her mother came in the kitchen door.

The Scotts lived in the small Connecticut town of Brighton, forty-five minutes from New York. Samantha's father worked for a medical supply company in the city, and often Mrs. Scott drove him to the station so she could use the car during the day.

"Did you have a good lesson today?" Samantha's father asked when they were settled at the dinner table.

"Mmm-hmmm." Samantha nodded. "We have a new girl in ballet class. She's from Russia. Her name is Lee-zinka." Samantha rolled the name around her tongue slowly and thoughtfully. "I've never heard that name before."

"That must be the family who moved into the Fox Mansion last week," Samantha's mother said. "I believe he's with the United Nations."

"That's right," Sam's father agreed. "They've come here from Moscow with their family. Mr. and Mrs. Petrovna. Grandmother came, too—along with the chauffeur. I met Mr. Petrovna in the drugstore the other night and introduced myself. He's a very friendly fellow."

"She's snooty!" Sam said, pushing her tuna casserole around her plate.

"How so?" her mother asked, looking at Mr. Scott with a raised eyebrow. Sam was not usually critical of people.

"Well," Sam said, wiping her mouth brusquely with her napkin, "she's a show-off!"

"Oh?" her mother said.

"Didn't you say she just came into your class today?" her father asked. "How can you judge her on such short acquaintance?"

"Well first," Sam said, "she walked on the floor and bowed to Miss Jan. It's called a *grande révérence* in ballet. We don't ever do that except at the end of the lesson." Sam's eyes looked up at the ceiling in disgust. "Then when she got to the *barre*, I turned to say 'Hi' to her, and she didn't even look at me!"

"It must be very hard for a girl that age to come into

a new country and try to make friends," Sam's mother pointed out. "It's amazing to me that she speaks English!"

"Everyone speaks English!" Samantha stated flatly.

"Think about it, Sam," said her father. "Would you be able to go to *her* country and speak Russian?"

"I think it would be nice to invite her to dinner some night after your lesson," her mother suggested.

"No way!" Samantha answered emphatically. "She'd never come! You know what, Mom? Lee-zinka wore a black leotard and pink tights, just like Miss Jan's teen class does." Sam's eyes sparkled mischievously. "I wish I could have some pink tights—maybe for my birthday—hint, hint!"

"We'll see, dear," replied her mother. "That's four weeks away. Right now, I think you should do your homework if you expect to watch TV tonight."

The week went by quickly. It was the night before her dance lesson when Sam realized her leotard and tights were still in her ballet box and she hadn't practiced once. She ran into the bathroom, quickly rinsed out her practice clothes, and hung them up to dry. They would be ready to put in her ballet box by morning. Luckily they didn't need ironing.

She would be getting new toe shoes soon—if she passed her exam, that is. Because Samantha and the other girls in her class had all shown such interest and talent in ballet, Miss Jan had always considered their class "special." She had planned for them all to go on toe together. But if any girl failed, she would fall behind the rest of the class.

As Samantha lay in bed, she stared off into space, lost for a moment in a dream world. As she often did, she envisioned herself in a white-and-silver *tutu*, a sparkling crown on her head, skimming lightly across the floor in her new toe shoes before an adoring audience. But this time the ballerina in her daydream kept changing to a different girl, one with blue eyes instead of brown, with dark hair pulled up halo fashion around her head, and wearing pink tights and pink toe shoes. It was Lizinka.

Samantha sighed and stretched out on her bed with her arms folded behind her head. The moonlight shone between the leaves of the oak tree outside her bedroom window, making intricate dance patterns on the ceiling. The nagging vision persisted, disturbing her reverie.

Why did she have to come to Brighton. And to *my* ballet class! she thought unhappily. I wish I could do double *tours* like Lizinka does! She pulled the sheet up under her chin, and scowling into the moonlit room, she whispered, "Guess I'm not as good as I thought I was."

Reluctantly Samantha admitted to herself that her world had always been a tight little orbit of family and friends. She had never before been threatened by something outside her world, and now she felt inadequate. "It isn't fair," she thought, pulling the covers tighter.

That night her sleep was troubled. She tossed and turned and when morning came, she had to be called twice before she finally dragged herself out of bed.

"'Morning, Mom," Samantha said as she kissed Mrs. Scott on the cheek, making her mother almost spill the juice on the tablecloth.

"'Morning, dear," her mother answered. "You look a little tired today."

"I couldn't sleep last night," Sam said, stretching her arms to the ceiling with a big yawn. In the light of day Lizinka didn't seem as much of a threat.

"Aren't you supposed to be working at your lessons each day now that you are preparing to go on toe? I haven't heard your practice record all week. Are you losing interest in your ballet?"

"Oh, no, Mom. You know I love it. It's just that—well, this new girl, Lee-zinka, she's so much better than I am."

"Do I see a green-eyed monster in the room?" her mother asked, smiling.

"Monster? Where?" Sam asked, looking around the room, then, seeing the smile on her mother's face, realized that she was being teased. "What do you mean?"

"Well, when we envy someone because she does something better than we do," her mother explained, "we say it's the green-eyed monster showing its ugly head. It's just an expression to indicate jealousy. Jealousy is not a very good trait unless you can turn it to your advantage."

"How do you mean?" asked Sam with a puzzled look. Sometimes her mother talked in riddles.

"Well," her mother continued, "a bit—a *little* bit— of envy sometimes can be a good thing, if it kindles a spark and makes you try to do better. It could even help you outshine your rival!"

Samantha chewed thoughtfully on a piece of toast. "Well, it isn't that I'm *jealous* of her, Mom," she answered, pausing a moment and staring off into space. "It's just that—I don't know how she can turn so fast!"

"Why don't you ask her? Maybe she has little wheels on her ballet slippers that help her spin." Her mother laughed.

"Oh, Mom, you're such a silly. Of course she doesn't—and I wouldn't *dare* ask her. She's not very friendly."

"Perhaps she's just shy. Sometimes people seem unfriendly and aloof when really they are afraid. She's in a strange country, you know. Why not try hard to be nice to her?"

Samantha finished her milk. "I'll try," she said, getting up from the table. "'Scuse me, Mom, it's getting late. I'd better get my ballet bag. And this time," she added, "I won't forget the elastic bands to tie up my hair!"

2

Lizinka Explains Russian Ballet

Samantha was ready for class. She wore her tights, leotard, and ballet slippers. This time her hair was in braids on the top of her head, except for a few little wispy tendrils that kept slipping out and curling at the nape of her neck. Miss Jan would be proud of her appearance today.

As she walked to the ballet *barre*, Sam noticed Lizinka talking to their ballet teacher, listening gravely to whatever Miss Jan was saying to her. Finally Lizinka nodded her head in agreement and followed Miss Jan to the center of the studio.

What was she going to do? Was she going to be promoted to another class? Samantha felt a guilty surge of joy at the possibility. Lizinka certainly danced better than anyone in this class. Watching her stand quietly beside Miss Jan, Samantha thought, She really does act stuck-up—or is it just shyness, like Mom said?

Just then Miss Jan called the class to attention, and after a minute or two the girls stopped talking and prepared for the *barre* work. But instead of going over to start the music as she usually did, Miss Jan put her arm around Lizinka's shoulders and said to the class, "Girls, I have asked Lizinka to tell us a bit about her ballet class in Russia. I thought you would enjoy hearing about it, and Lizinka has agreed. Why don't you girls sit on the floor and be comfortable? Go ahead, Lizinka." Miss Jan smiled encouragingly.

Lizinka stood tall and straight. Her hair was braided and coiled about her head as before. She did not smile at the class, but a faint flush of color touched her cheeks.

"Thank you, Madame," she said in a soft, quiet voice. "Excuse me, I mean Miss Jan." Lizinka had an accent that sounded strange. The other girls glanced quickly at one another and over to their teacher to see how she reacted, but Miss Jan did not change her expression.

"Yes. Well—your customs here in America, they are quite different from ours." The Russian girl spoke haltingly, searching briefly for the English words. "The first thing I notice is that you do not stand when your *maîtresse de ballet* enters the classroom. We show very great respect to our teachers by always rising and giving them com-plete attention."

Lizinka's grammar was perfect, but the way she rolled her *r*'s around her tongue and occasionally accented certain words on the wrong syllable made the girls in Sam's class very uncomfortable. They had never heard this particular accent before from someone their own age.

"When," Lizinka continued, "our teacher calls the class, 'Ready to begin,' we would not *dream* of talking! It is considered very bad manners to do that. If we wish to continue with our lessons, we had better obey!" The class looked at one another sheepishly. Someone giggled nervously and quickly stifled it, making a funny gurgling sound. Suddenly the whole class broke into gales of laughter.

Startled, Lizinka quickly looked at Miss Jan, expecting her to be angry. Instead, the teacher joined in the laughter with the class. Then, noticing Lizinka's discomfort, Miss Jan quickly went over to her. Taking her hand, she said, "We aren't laughing at you, dear, or your customs. It is just that our classes are more informal. Please tell us more. We really are interested, aren't we, class?"

"Yes, oh yes!" echoed the class, settling down to listen.

"Yes. So," Lizinka went on, trying to regain her composure, "when we are very young we are picked to go to school where ballet is a daily part of our lives. We are examined in the second grade, and if we seem to have real po-tential for the dance, we are placed in the Bolshoi for Children. This is a *great* honor and a dream come true!" Lizinka's face lit up, and her eyes brimmed over with tears. She seemed lonesome for her old school.

Watching her, Samantha felt a twinge of sympathy. "I must make an effort to be more friendly," she told herself firmly, pushing the angry thoughts of the night before from her mind.

The class looked away self-consciously, pretending not to see the big tear that splashed down over Lizinka's nose.

"You see, class," Miss Jan said, "the Bolshoi in Moscow is world famous." Miss Jan looked dreamily off into space. "I remember my visit to the USSR a few years back. I was actually admitted to observe a class conducted by the great ballet master Yuri Grigorovich!" She smiled to herself. "When I met Director Vladimir Yolubin, he clicked his heels and bent low, and then he kissed my hand! They are indeed more formal than we are here in America!"

Miss Jan smiled again; then she continued, "The Bolshoi is a magnificent building with an imposing statue on top of the main entrance. The statue is a golden chariot, drawn by three horses and driven by

Apollo, the Patron of the Arts. The building itself is huge, with many practice halls and elegant ballrooms with sparkling chandeliers and red velvet furnishings. The children have a special classroom where they practice, and at times they are allowed to go into the theater to watch the rehearsals onstage. Being so close to all this culture makes the young dancer very aware of the hard work needed to become a truly great ballerina. Right, Lizinka?"

"That is true, Miss Jan," replied the Russian girl. Miss Jan had given her just enough time to regain her composure, and Lizinka was delighted that her teacher had seen her school in Russia. "When we are picked to go to school at the Bolshoi," she continued, "we know that those who don't work hard and make steady progress have to leave. There is a long waiting list of children who would *love* to take our places.

"Time is not to be wasted on lazy children. This is a part of a regular school, you see. We have reading and math as you do in your public schools, but along with that we have to study about the history of ballet. We must take written tests on ballet terms. Our examinations are both written and spoken, and they are also on techniques at the *barre*, which is most important. If we do not keep up with all of our work to the satisfaction of our teacher, we are expelled."

"Wow!" said the class in one breath, looking wide-eyed at one another.

"So the competition is keen in a school like that,"

said Miss Jan. "The demands are great, and it takes discipline of both mind and body to remain there. Right, dear?"

"Oh yes," answered Lizinka excitedly, happy to have someone understand her way of living. "You see," she said, the words coming easily and tumbling out like water rushing over pebbles, "we don't dance for fun and recreation as you seem to do here in America. This is serious study. If we don't know our lesson, we are sharply reprimanded. It is embarrassing and it is shameful. We are constantly reminded that if we don't want to work and take advantage of this privilege, which is *given to us by the state*, there are others waiting who will!"

But it sure brought results, thought Samantha. No wonder she is such a good dancer. Lizinka had really had to work at it. Samantha felt a twinge of conscience at her own laziness and again made a silent promise to herself to do better in the future.

"That is so interesting, Lizinka," Miss Jan said. "Is there anything else that makes our classes here different from yours?"

"Ahhhhh, well," she said thoughtfully, "there *is* one thing I haven't seen in this studio yet."

"Oh?" questioned Miss Jan, looking around the studio. "What is that? We have a ballet *barre*— mirrors—mats—what else is missing here?"

Samantha thought she could sense a slight tension in her teacher. Miss Jan took great pride in her shiny new studio with colorful Degas prints on the wall. Now was this newcomer telling her there was something missing? The class sensed the coolness in Miss Jan's voice and sat up straight, eager to hear what Lizinka would say. Miss Jan was patient and sweet most of the time, but every once in a while, if she felt somone was trying to downgrade her school—*beware!*

"What is missing?" asked Miss Jan again. Her chin tipped up, and her eyes appraised her new student steadily.

"The switch," said Lizinka, looking her new teacher right in the eye. "The ballet switch, such as Madame Barakova used on our ankles when we did not turn out properly. I have not seen a switch in here."

Miss Jan let out a sigh of relief, and a kind look came into her eyes. "And you won't see one here, either," she said, going over to the Russian girl and gently placing an arm around her shoulders.

"So you see, class, I wanted Lizinka to tell you about her school for two reasons: One, because it is interesting to hear about how other countries teach ballet. You will realize that no matter where you go in the world, the technique is basically the same, and the language of ballet is always French.

"The second reason—and this is almost more important to you—is that I could sense a feeling of frustration and disappointment in this class last week when you saw Lizinka do her double *tours*. You were wondering why Lizinka is much better than you are. Now you know why that is. She has had lessons each *day*, and you have had only one lesson a *week*. She has had a great deal more training than you have.

"Don't be disappointed in yourselves. I'm not. Perhaps, though, we can learn from one another. From the Russian school we learn that daily work is necessary in order to become truly great ballerinas. This is why it is so important for you to do your practicing at home each day. On the other hand, we here in America can show Lizinka the joy we get from dancing—which she seems to have missed.

"Now, some more news," Miss Jan continued. "Even though Lizinka is more advanced in technique than you are, she, too, is eleven years old. Even in Russia no one starts toe work before then. So she will remain in this class and go *en pointe* when you do. That is, of course, *if* you all pass your examinations." She looked piercingly at each one of the girls.

"Over to the *barre*, class, and let's really work hard from now on. Exams are just two weeks away, and we must make the most of our time."

The class moved quietly to the ballet *barre*, thoughts of the Bolshoi and Lizinka on their minds. More seriously than ever before they all did their *pliés* and *ports de bras*, moving on to more difficult combinations. The only sound in the studio was the classical music and Miss Jan's voice quietly giving directions and counting. It was almost as though the class had crossed the ocean to Russia, and for a full half hour twelve young ballerinas worked as hard as they knew how. It was a beautiful sight to see. Miss Jan looked very proud when the class was over.

As Samantha went by Lizinka, she smiled at her and said, "See you next week!"

Lizinka nodded briefly as she ran out of the studio door and got into the big black chauffeur-driven diplomatic limousine that was waiting for her.

3

Sam Offers Friendship

That night at dinner, Sam told her mother and father all about the ballet school in Russia.

"Just think," said Samantha excitedly, "the teacher uses a little switch on their ankles if they don't turn out properly."

"What do you mean, turn out properly?" her father asked.

"Well, in ballet," Sam began earnestly, happy to be able to teach her father something for a change, since he always knew about everything, "there are five positions of the feet. In first position, you have to put your heels together and turn out the whole leg all the way up to the hip socket. It's really hard to do, but 'the better the turnout, the better the dancer.'" Sam, with a twinkle in her eye, mimicked Miss Jan to perfection.

"You mean in Russia the teacher uses a switch on the ankles to make lazy students work harder?" asked her mother.

"Yep, that's right. That's what Lee says," replied Samantha.

"Oho, so now it's Lee, is it?" Her mother laughed. "Did she tell you it was all right to call her that?"

"Noooo—she didn't," admitted Sam. "But why not? Everyone calls me Sam, don't they?"

"Well, you'd better ask her," her mother suggested. "Some people are very touchy about nicknames."

"Really! I never knew that," Sam replied. "No one ever asked me!"

"That's because we started calling you Sam the day you were born—so you really had no choice in the matter. You don't mind it, do you?"

Sam leaned her elbows on the table, chin in hand, and gazed thoughtfully into space.

"Samantha—Sam Scott." She said the name over softly to herself several times. "Ugh! That doesn't sound like a girl," she said, wrinkling her nose distastefully. "Not much like a ballerina's name should sound."

Her braids were still on the top of her head from

dancing class, but now one stuck out of the elastic band like a little devil's horn. Her brown eyes looked mischievously back at her father across the table as she thought for a moment.

"Allegro—Allegra. When Miss Jan has us do our dance steps to fast music, that's what she calls it. I think Allegra Scott would be better for a ballerina— don't you think so, Dad?" She tossed her head and before he could answer, added, "That sounds a lot better than *Sam* Scott, that's for sure!"

"First of all," her mother said, snatching Sam out of her dream world, "before changing your name, why not change your shoes and put on your ballet slippers and do some practicing? What do you think of that idea?"

"I agree," said her father. "I'd like to see that *barre* that you begged me to put up in your room get some use."

"Gotta call Naomi first, then I will, Dad," Sam said as she got up from the kitchen table.

Her call to Naomi was brief.

"Hi, Naomi," Sam said into the receiver. "What did you think of Lee-zinka's speech today in class?"

"I was just telling my mom and dad about it at dinner tonight." Naomi's voice diminished to a whisper. "I'll tell you what they said when I see you tomorrow, okay?"

"What do you mean?" Sam asked, puzzled. "What did they say?"

"Never mind now, I've gotta go do the dishes. See you on the way to school tomorrow. I'll be waiting for you." And with that she hung up the phone.

Samantha thoughtfully tapped the receiver with her fingertips. Then, heaving a big, impatient sigh, she pushed aside her desire to call back. Naomi always loved to make a mystery of everything, so it was probably nothing at all. She'd just have to wait until school the next day. Right now she'd better do her homework!

In her bedroom, after doing her homework, Sam put on her practice record and turned on the record player. Then, for a full half hour, she did her exercises. She remembered watching the teen-age class just before her own dance lesson. How diligently they worked at the *barre*! Beads of perspiration on their foreheads, their muscles actually trembling as they extended their legs high above their heads and held them there. Never a murmur of protest came from them. Samantha tried to display the same kind of self-discipline. Her body ached from the effort, but she felt pleased with herself.

Then, running the hot water, she added pink bubble bath and sank into the bathtub with a happy sigh. The bubbles sparkled and glistened in the light—like a pink *tutu*, Samantha thought sleepily.

Putting on her nightgown, she made a promise to herself before going to sleep. Each day, without fail, she would practice for at least half an hour. She might not be as good as Lizinka, but that didn't mean she couldn't give her a little competition. With their toe shoes, they would both be starting out on a new adventure. Samantha did not give up easily. She loved to dance and would try her best to make Miss Jan proud of her.

"And *next* lesson," she thought, feeling very satisfied with herself, "I'll ask Lizinka if I can call her Lee."

Naomi was waiting by her gate when Samantha rounded the corner on her way to school the next day. Naomi was a spirited girl with a flair for comedy and a love of gossip. She was an only child of older parents who doted on her and spoiled her. Her freckles, "golden kisses of the sun," her mother called them, splashed across her turned-up nose and framed her green eyes, which never missed a trick. Samantha loved to be around her because she kept things humming, but Naomi's sharp tongue made her uncomfortable at times.

As Samantha approached her friend on this particular morning, she could see that Naomi was bursting with news. Her short, curly red hair sprang from the roots of her head like little wire springs. When Naomi saw Samantha, she ran to meet her.

"What's going on, Naomi?" Sam asked, laughing at her friend. Naomi was chewing gum so fast her dimples flashed in and out like blinking Christmas-tree lights. Sometimes Sam got so engrossed in watching the dimples, she didn't even hear what Naomi was saying. But today was different; Sam was very curious because she knew Naomi was talking about Lizinka.

"My mother says," Naomi said very fast, "it isn't fair to let Lizinka be in our class. She's too advanced, and it makes *us* look bad. My mother thinks it could discourage us from trying!

"Besides," she continued, lowering her voice to a whisper, "my father says you can never trust a Russian!"

This was not the first time Sam had heard Naomi's family say things about foreigners. They had gone through this before, when a Chinese family had come to town. Remembering her own parents' advice at that time—"Don't judge people just because they are different from you"—Sam quickly changed the subject and began talking about something else.

The next Monday afternoon Sam felt confident as she worked out at the *barre* in class. She had kept her promise to herself and practiced faithfully each day. Miss Jan nodded and smiled as she watched her perform.

"Next week will be our final exam, class," she said. "Keep up the good work."

After the *grande révérence,* the class was over. Since Sam's mother was going to pick her up after class, Sam was waiting outside when Lizinka came out and headed toward her limousine.

"It's now or never," said Sam to herself. "Mom said I should be friendly—so here goes!"

Turning to the Russian girl, she grinned and said, "My name's Samantha, but my friends call me Sam. Do you mind if I call you Lee?"

Lizinka was buckling her ballet bag with the very important-looking emblem and the Russian letters on it, which Sam could not read. She looked up, startled. She hesitated; then looking back at Sam with eyes like two chunks of blue ice, she replied, "In my country nicknames are used among friends and family. I do not believe we can be considered more than mere acquaintances." And without so much as a wave of her hand, she got into her limousine and rode away.

Samantha was flabbergasted! She must be mistaken! She couldn't have heard right! The words had such a strong impact on her it was almost as if Lizinka had physically hit her. For a moment she actually hurt. From a distance she heard her mother's voice calling, "Sam, Sam, what's the matter?" Only then did she realize she was on the sidewalk outside the studio and her mother was calling from the car.

As Sam hopped into the front seat beside her mother, hot tears welled up in her eyes, and she blinked hard to push them back, not wanting to talk about what had just happened. But nothing escaped

her mother's watchful eye, and after driving for a few seconds, she said softly, "What is it, honey? What's troubling you?"

Hearing her mother's gentle voice, and safe in the knowledge that no one else could see her, Samantha put both hands over her face and sobbed quietly, a hurt kind of cry. Mrs. Scott pulled the car over to the side of the road and took Sam into her arms, letting her cry until it was over.

Samantha, taking a deep breath, exhaled slowly and said, "I'm all right, Mom. It's just that my feelings were hurt. I spoke to her like you said I should and tried to be friendly to her. I told her my name and asked if I could call her Lee. She looked at me so funny, like I had said something wrong, and when she ran to her car, she said something like, 'Nicknames are used by friends and family and we are only—*acquaintances.*' "

Mrs. Scott looked at her daughter for a moment and, brushing Sam's hair back from her wet cheeks, said seriously, "That was rude. Perhaps it would be better to let her make the next move. It would seem she doesn't want to be friends."

Samantha took another deep breath and let it out slowly. The sigh ended with a little hiccup that sounded like the snap of a twig. Her eyes opened wide, and her hand quickly covered her mouth. As she looked at her mother, they both burst into laughter, tensions vanishing.

"Now there," said her mother, "that's that. Let's go visit your Aunt Em—I'll bet she'll have some cookies and milk. Try to forget the whole thing."

Sure enough, when they got to her Aunt Emmy's house, the delicious smell of molasses cookies greeted them as they came up onto the porch. When they opened the kitchen door, they could see a plate on the table piled high with golden cookies.

If Aunt Emmy noticed Samantha's red-rimmed eyes, she didn't mention it. Giving Sam a big squeeze, she went directly to the refrigerator for the pitcher of milk and poured a glass for Sam. The three of them sat around the kitchen table visiting and chatting about all sorts of things, and before they knew it, the whole plateful of cookies was gone— most of them eaten by Sam. Crying sure gives me an appetite, thought Sam.

Not a word was said about her upsetting experience, and Sam was glad. She had tried to be friends and had been rejected. Now, as her mother said, Lizinka would have to make the next move. Besides, Sam had work to do. Her exam was next week, and she would have to practice hard each day to be in condition for it.

Suddenly she realized that it was possible that Miss Jan might not put her on toe this year! She had given them all fair warning that there was no real promise of it. And after watching Lizinka, Samantha was bewildered and very unsure of her ability. Miss

Jan had stressed the necessity for daily practice, and Sam had not always practiced as much as she should. She wasn't about to be humiliated in front of Lizinka again. She could hardly wait to get home to practice. She simply must not fail this exam!

4

The Exam

"So this is the big day," her mother said as she helped Sam zip up the back of her dress.

"Uh-huh!" Sam said excitedly. Then she looked at her mother searchingly. "What if I don't pass, Mom?"

"Sam, honey, I suppose if you don't, there will be a good reason for it. Your class has been working hard for quite a while, and I've been very pleased with your practice at home lately. But if Miss Jan thinks you should wait another year, until your back and legs are stronger, try not to be too disappointed."

"Oh, I just can't wait another year!" moaned Sam.

Mrs. Scott could sense her need for encouragement.

"Oh, honey," she said, tears stinging her own eyes, "you'll do just fine. I'm sure of it!" Drawing her daughter close to her, she kissed the top of her head. Then, holding her at arm's length and looking deep into her eyes, she said, "Come right home after your lesson, promise? I'll be anxious to hear all about it."

"I will, Mom," Sam promised.

"And good luck!" her mother said.

Grabbing her dance bag, Samantha ran out the door and down the porch steps, almost falling as she tripped over the last step.

"Hey, careful," her mother called. "I thought dancers were supposed to be graceful!"

Laughing, Sam waved over her shoulder and ran to meet her friends.

Classes seemed to drag on endlessly. Samantha usually loved English, but today she could not seem to keep her mind on it. Math was *always* a problem. She never could understand it, and today of all days it was a disaster! Mr. Heino, her math teacher, asked how many digits she should move a decimal point, and she answered absentmindedly, "Three *pliés*." The class roared, and she felt like hiding under her desk; she was so embarrassed. But finally the bell rang, and the school day was over.

Gathering her things together, she joined some of

her ballet-class friends who, talking excitedly, teased her about her faux pas in math class as they headed for the studio.

The teen class was in session as they arrived, so they quietly went into the dressing room to change. Her classmates seemed less noisy than usual. Sam looked in the mirror to pin her hair up. "I hope I pass," she whispered to her reflection. Then she crossed the shiny studio floor and stood waiting at the ballet *barre* for instructions.

Miss Jan looked at the twelve girls. Each one stood poised, with her hair piled high on her head, ready for the big exam that would determine whether she could go *en pointe* this year.

"*Pré-pa-ra-tion!*" Miss Jan said in a clear, precise voice, and every girl was ready. Slowly and methodically she put them through their *barre* work —walking up and down, checking the line of the back, the strength of the legs, the stretch of the foot.

Then it was time for the center work.

"This is it!" thought Samantha. "If my balance isn't good, I won't make it!"

"Feet in second position, class," Miss Jan said. Then, starting the record player, she counted in a slow, steady voice: "*Plié* two three four, up six seven eight. *Relevé* two three four, lower six seven eight."

Never before had the studio been so quiet. There was complete concentration as each girl stared straight ahead, remembering to lean ever so slightly forward to hold her balance better.

Beads of perspiration stood out on Sam's upper lip as she tightened her leg, derriere, and stomach muscles and remembered to keep her shoulders pressed down and relaxed. One of the girls lost her balance on a *relevé*, but no one looked around. They were all trying not to let it happen to them!

Plié and *relevé*. Down and up they went, as Miss Jan walked around, looking each girl over very carefully. Sam glanced at Lizinka, who was right beside her and looked as self-assured as usual. She *would*, thought Sam, with an angry glance at the ceiling.

At long last Miss Jan said, "Relax, girls. I want to talk to you for a few minutes. Please sit on the floor."

Oh dear, thought Sam, she looks so serious. Maybe none of us passed.

"I want my class to be well informed, so if anyone questions you about toe work, you can answer intelligently. Can you tell me why you are not allowed to go on toe before age ten and preferably eleven?"

"I know, I know!" said a vivacious girl named Lisa. "It's because the bones in our toes are not developed enough until then. It's just car-ti—cartilage."

"Very good, Lisa," Miss Jan said. "Feel the tip of your nose and tell me—what does it feel like?"

The Exam

"Feels like Silly Putty," volunteered Michelle, grinning impishly.

"Exactly!" agreed Miss Jan. "That's the way your toes are until the bone is formed. Now at age ten," she went on, "there is a definite bone formation, especially in the first metatarsal and big-toe joint, which is where most of your toe work is done." Taking off her ballet slipper, Miss Jan pointed to her big toe and the toe next to it. "The heel bones are well developed, which means the arch structure will support your foot properly as you do your dance steps."

Samantha squirmed impatiently and looked at Naomi with a raised eyebrow. She had heard this all before. They all listened attentively, however, knowing Miss Jan was very serious. Could it be that she was going to suggest they wait another year? Samantha felt her heart hit the bottom of her ballet slippers.

"You are all around eleven, which gives you an extra year's bone growth, and that is very good. If you had gone on toe *before* age ten, you could have injured your feet for life.

"Another question: Why is it so important to be able to balance? Can you tell us, Sam?"

"It's because," Sam answered quickly, "if we can't hold our balance firmly, it means we have not learned to place our body weight properly over our feet." Miss Jan had been warning them about this for a whole year.

"Right again!" their teacher said. "And if you can't place your body weight properly over your feet in ballet slippers, how could you possibly do it in toe shoes? Right, class?"

"Right!" echoed the class, anxious to please.

"I had planned to wait until next week to tell you who had passed the exam. . . ."

"Ohhhhhhhhhh!" the disappointed sighs echoed deeply through the studio.

"But"—Miss Jan smiled understandingly—"I am so pleased with each one of you, I won't keep you in suspense another second. You will all go on toe as soon as your toe shoes arrive! Good work, girls!"

"We made it! We made it!" they shouted, jumping up from the floor where they had been sitting. They started laughing, hugging, and clapping. Such a clatter of sounds filled the studio that Miss Jan raised her hand for silence.

"Shhhhh—quiet, girls. Your work has just begun. You will find when you put on those toe shoes that it is harder than it looks. Remember, you will not float away in them," she warned them for the umpteenth time.

"We know—we know!" They laughed. But nothing could dampen their spirits. They all had worked hard toward this for several years, and they felt very happy now that the tension was past. They all acted happy— all except Lizinka, who remained very cool and aloof. Thanking Miss Jan matter-of-factly, she went into the dressing room, put on her coat and hat, and went outside to the limousine, which was waiting for her. Samantha, standing for a moment to one side of the hubbub, watched her go. How can she be so calm about everything? Sam wondered. She never smiled—she never showed any emotion. Couldn't she at least be happy *today*, of all days?

Naomi had been watching Lizinka too, and as if she had read Sam's mind, she broke into a grin as she popped a stick of gum into her mouth. She always had gum handy for after class. Miss Jan had fits if they chewed in class.

Naomi struck an aloof pose, and sticking her freckled nose into the air, she looked for all the world like Lizinka. Imitating her Russian accent to perfection, she said, "So. Well. I must leave you peasants and to my sho-fur limousine—go."

All the girls in the dressing room broke into gales of laughter. Sam joined in the laughter, but not without a nagging feeling of guilt. Although Sam had been deeply hurt by Lizinka, she found it difficult to bear a grudge for long. Not to be friends with someone troubled her deep down inside.

She was too happy and excited to wonder about Lizinka for very long, however. She must hurry home and tell her mother the good news!

That evening at dinner, Sam was so excited that her father suggested she simmer down before she boiled over!

"Good girl! I knew you could do it!" Mr. Scott boasted when she told her parents of her successful exam.

"Did everyone pass?" her mother asked, relieved to see Sam's happy face.

"Well, it was so funny. Everything was going along fine, see?" Sam was gesturing more than usual, she was so excited. "After our *barre* work Miss Jan said to get into the center and put our feet into second position for our *pliés*. We all knew she was going to see how our balance was—'cause if it wasn't steady, we were not putting our weight over our feet correctly and so were not ready for toe work." Sam opened her eyes wide and took a deep breath. Holding back a giggle, she said, "Naomi lost her balance! I didn't know who it was until later but I could hear a shuffling of feet behind me. And then in the dressing room Naomi told us about it. Wow, was she nervous! Miss Jan just ignored it, though. Naomi really is a good dancer."

"I'll bet the class was excited," her mother said.

"All except Lizinka," Sam said. "I don't understand how she can be so calm. You know, she just nodded to Miss Jan and thanked her, then went into the dressing room, put on her coat, and left!" Sam thought it best not to tell about Naomi's imitation.

"Not everyone shows emotions the same way, you know," her father said. "Have you tried to be friends with her as your mother suggested?"

Sam looked quickly at her mother. Apparently she had kept their secret and not told her father about her attempt to make friends with Lizinka. Before Sam had a chance to answer, her mother said, "Can you stand another surprise in one day, Sam?"

"What do you mean?" Sam asked.

"Well, Dad and I thought, since next Monday is your birthday, we would give you a party this year."

"Oh, wow!" Sam jumped up from the table to give them each a hug. "That would be super!"

"As soon as we finish dessert, we can make our plans while we clear the table and wash the dishes," her mother said.

They had Jell-O for dessert, and it slid down very fast for Sam. Her mother and father were discussing politics when they looked over to see Sam noisily scraping the goblet to show that she was finished. Laughing, they stood up. "I'll let you two make your plans," Mr. Scott said. "I'll watch the news. Let me know what I can do to help."

"Great, Dad!" Sam said, bustling about to clear the table.

"The autumn weather is still so lovely. Would you like to have a barbecue out on the patio?" her mother asked as she started washing the dishes. "Or would you rather have an indoor party?"

"I think a barbecue would be lots of fun!" Sam agreed.

"I thought you could have it after your dancing lesson Monday, and you could play croquet and badminton—probably for the last time before it snows." Obviously Mrs. Scott had given it some previous thought.

"Then we could have hot dogs and hamburgers when we get hungry." Sam's eyes sparkled. She always got excited about parties.

"And I will be the cook!" her father announced, coming into the kitchen and hearing Sam's last remark. "No one cooks hamburgers quite like I do." He threw out his chest proudly.

"Except when you try to beat Mom at badminton and forget to turn them," Sam teased him—reminding him of the last barbecue, with Aunt Emmy and their cousins.

"Well, we don't talk about that!" Her father laughed.

"If you don't stop drying that dish, you'll wipe away the design," her mother teased. "I'll finish up here. You sit down and write a list of girls you'd like to invite. You can tell the girls about it at school tomorrow."

Sam sat at the kitchen table with a memo pad and pencil and wrote rapidly for a few minutes. Her mother finished putting away the dishes, often glancing over to see how Sam was getting along. She could see her daughter counting the names on her list and scratching out first one, then another—only to write the same name again.

Finally, putting her elbows on the table and her chin in her hands, Sam said, "Y'know, Mom, I never realized it till now, but all my best friends are in ballet class!"

"It's really not that surprising," her mother said. "You are all about the same age and have taken lessons together for so long. People with the same interests are more likely to become friends. Now leave your list and say good night to Dad. Then pop into bed. It's getting late."

Putting down the pencil, Sam gave her mother a quick hug. "I'll tell the girls tomorrow. I can't wait till Monday. Thanks, Mom." And off she went to get ready for bed.

Mrs. Scott picked up the memo pad with the list of names, smiling to herself as she saw Sam's many erasures and pencil scratchings. Then she went in to talk to her husband.

It was about ten o'clock when she started up the stairs to bed. As she got to Sam's door, she thought she saw a light under it; then she heard a click. Listening for a second, she was sure she heard footsteps. She knocked very lightly and whispered, "Are you all right, Sam?"

No answer. A creaking of the rocking chair puzzled Mrs. Scott. Softly she opened the door and looked in. Sam was not in her bed. The moonlight streamed into the room through the open window. Huddled in the rocker and gazing out the window at the starlit night sat Samantha, her long nightgown tucked under her feet. Concerned, her mother hurried over to her.

"What's the matter, dear? Don't you feel well?"

"Oh, Mom," Sam said mournfully, "I just can't sleep. I keep thinking of Lizinka and how she will feel when she finds out she is the only one from my ballet class who isn't invited to the party."

"I thought, Sam," her mother said softly, "that you agreed it would be better for her to make the next move to be friends."

"If I wait for that time, we'll *never* be friends." Sam's bare foot gave a push, and the chair rocked swiftly back and forth. The moonlight shone across Sam's worried face.

Sam's mother led her back to bed and tucked her in. Kissing the top of her head, she whispered, "Go to sleep, honey. I'll call Mrs. Petrovna in the morning."

5

Eleven Years Old

Sam liked to wake to the warm autumn sun shining across her bed in the morning, so she kept her shade up at night. Opening her eyes, she sprang out of bed and ran to look out the window. It was a good day!

"Happy birthday, eleven-year-old," her mother greeted her as she came into the kitchen. "Dad said to give you a big kiss for him and said he'd be here in time to cook the hot dogs and hamburgers for your party tonight."

"It's not going to rain!" Sam said, hugging her mother. "We can have my party outdoors on the patio. It will be such fun! All the girls are coming after dancing school." The words came tumbling out over one another. Mrs. Scott wondered how Samantha would sit through school all day.

"Did you get Lizinka's mother on the phone last night, Mom?" Sam asked anxiously. Sam had not actually spoken to Lizinka since the upsetting day when she asked to call her Lee, but she felt quite sure that if they had a chance to talk, they could iron out their differences. At least Sam was willing to make the effort once again to become friends.

Sam's mother had been trying to get Mrs. Petrovna all week, but no one had answered. Finally, the night before, she had got through to Lizinka's house. A woman's voice with a heavy Russian accent had answered, *"Dawbry vehchuhr."* Mrs. Scott had decided the woman who had answered was probably the maid.

"She is for a few days gone away," the woman had said in reply to Mrs. Scott's request to speak to Mrs. Petrovna. It was very hard to make her understand about the barbecue. Mrs. Scott finally was able to explain that the girls were in the same ballet class.

"Lizinka come to ber-ta-day party, *da?"* she had replied. After many attempts, Mrs. Scott finally seemed to make the woman understand by using the word *dinner* several times. She gave her their address and said Lizinka should come after ballet class and be picked up at about eight o'clock.

"So," Mrs. Scott said, "I think maybe she'll be here for your party. *If* the woman got the message straight. Only let's not worry about it. She has been invited. Now have a happy day, and I'll see you all after ballet class."

This was the day the girls were to be fitted for toe shoes, so nothing seemed normal. They each had to have imprints made of their feet, and tell the shoe man who was measuring them their usual street size, so that the toe shoes would be just right—not too tight or too loose. Like figure skates or ski boots, they couldn't be bought to grow into.

Lizinka arrived late for class. Everyone else had already been fitted for her toe shoes and was going to the *barre.* Miss Jan said she would have to be fitted for her shoes after class.

As soon as the lesson was over, Miss Jan called Lizinka, so Sam did not get a chance to ask if she was coming to the party. The other girls went into the dressing room and put on their jeans and shirts for the barbecue. They went wild over a top that Lisa had tie-dyed; another shirt, which Debby wore, had the names of all the girls who had gone to a pajama party at her house last summer. The girls had also brought gaily wrapped birthday gifts for Sam.

On the way to Sam's house, with the colorful packages under their arms, they laughed about being fitted to toe shoes, comparing notes as to who had the biggest feet.

"How come Lizinka isn't with us?" Naomi asked, looking slyly at the other girls and then back to Samantha. "I thought you said you had invited her."

"We did!" Samantha said, her heart beating hard. "My mother isn't sure that the maid understood her, though. She doesn't speak English very well."

"I think that's dumb!" Naomi said explosively. "They can't be very bright if they don't know how to speak the English language." Her dimples flashed in and out as she chewed excitedly on her gum.

"Just a minute, Naomi; would you know how to speak *Russian* if you went to Russia?" Samantha interrupted Naomi, not quite remembering where she had heard those words before but finding it necessary to defend Lizinka.

"Well, never mind now," Naomi rationalized, not really knowing how to answer that one and still come out ahead. "Let's just forget it." So, too excited to let anything spoil their day, they did just that.

As they rounded the bend and Sam's yard came into view, a festive sight met their eyes. Japanese lanterns were strung from one tree to another. Balloons of all colors hung from the branches. Mrs. Scott and Aunt Em were sipping cool drinks on the patio, looking a bit weary from the decorating spree. Depositing their gifts on the table and flinging themselves on the lawn, the excited girls admired the decorations and gratefully accepted the lemonade offered them.

Lisa and Debby played a game of croquet while the others watched, taking sides and cheering them on. Sam played badminton with Michelle, then sat down with a glass of lemonade. While enjoying it all, Sam still kept glancing up the street, anxiously waiting for Lizinka's arrival. Or wasn't she going to come? The table was set with a red-and-white checked table- cloth. Chips and pickles, along with paper plates, were being put on the table by Mrs. Scott and Aunt Emmy. There were relishes, mustard, onions, ketchup, and mayonnaise—all the fixings anyone could possibly want to "doctor up" hamburgers and hot dogs.

"Almost ready," signaled Mr. Scott, who had come home from work and put on his big barbecue apron and hat.

"Shouldn't we wait for Lizinka, Mom?"

"Honey," her mother said, arranging paper plates, "she probably didn't even get the message. You remember I said I had trouble getting the maid to understand me. Just forget about it and enjoy your birthday party, okay?"

"I am, Mom. I'm having a wonderful time." But she frowned a little as she turned to go back to her friends. It was beginning to get dusky. The lanterns were lit, and the patio and lawn glowed warmly.

Just then a big black limousine rounded the corner, slowly drove up the street, and came to a halt in front of Sam's house.

"It's Lizinka!" cried Sam happily.

"Lizinka's here!" echoed the girls in loud whispers. Mr. and Mrs. Scott exchanged glances; then Sam's mother looked at her and smiled reassuringly.

But no one got out of the car. Everyone waited. They couldn't see anyone in the backseat. The chauffeur was talking to someone, but still the car door did not open. Then very, very slowly, the black limousine started moving away from Sam's house.

Quick as an arrow, Sam ran out to the street.

"Lizinka! Lizinka!" she called after the slowly moving car.

It stopped.

It backed up.

It came to a halt by Sam. Crouched in the corner of the backseat, looking very, very small, was Lizinka.

"I thought you weren't coming!" Sam yelled through the closed window.

After some seconds Lizinka opened the window. She spoke in a quiet, uncertain little voice. "Nanatasha, that's my grandmamma, said it was a dinner party. Mamma, she is away."

"I'm glad you're here," Samantha said politely, feeling the need to be formal with her foreign guest.

"I can't come to your party. I'm sorry. I'm not dressed right." Lizinka glanced quickly past Sam and over to the lawn, where the other girls played in their jeans and shirts.

Then for the first time Samantha noticed that Lizinka was wearing a beautiful blue ruffled party dress and shiny patent-leather slippers. A large blue ribbon was in her dark-brown hair, which now hung loosely over her shoulders. She looked like a little girl, quite different from the poised young lady in ballet class.

Not quite knowing how to handle the situation, Sam turned to call out to her mother, only to find that her father was right behind her. Apparently he had heard the conversation and was gallantly ready to put Lizinka at ease.

Opening the car door, he reached into the backseat and helped Lizinka out. Smiling at her, he said, "I met your dad at the drugstore a few weeks ago. We had a nice little visit. How do you like it here in America?"

Samantha didn't even hear the answer, so aware was she of Lizinka's discomfort. Helping this shy, stiff girl, who was unfamiliar with casual American ways, was a challenge Sam accepted. With her father on one side, she moved to the other and impulsively reached for Lizinka's hand. Only then did she realize that Lizinka was holding some wild flowers—black-eyed Susans and Queen Anne's lace—*upside down.* The upside-down flowers seemed odd, but Sam said nothing and led Lizinka to her mother, who had started toward them.

"Mom, this is Lizinka!" Sam said.

Smiling, her mother put out her hand, and Lizinka took it. She made a quick little curtsy and handed Mrs. Scott the flowers, saying formally, "How do you do?"

"Isn't it super that Lizinka could come?" Sam said brightly to all her friends. "Her mother's away and her nana thought this was a dinner party. Isn't Lizinka's dress beautiful?"

"Oh, wow! It's lovely!" they said, all sensing Lizinka's embarrassment.

"I feel like a slob," said Naomi, and they all burst into laughter.

Sam, who was holding Lizinka's hand, could feel the tenseness vanish. The Russian girl looked from one to another, and suddenly a big smile came over her usually solemn face.

"Get your plates, girls. The hamburgers and hot dogs are ready," said Mr. Scott. His timing was perfect. They all made a mad scramble for the barbecue and then back to the table for the fixings. Lizinka, puzzled but game, joined in the fun.

Finally, it was time for the cake. Aunt Emmy had made it, and a lovely ballerina stood *en pointe* on the top. The dancer was wearing a tiny silver tiara and a silver-and-white *tutu*, almost exactly like the one Sam had dreamed about. Sam wondered how her Aunt Emmy had known this!

After singing "Happy Birthday," they ate their cake and ice cream. Then Sam opened her presents.

She received games, a dance poster, and an autograph pillow for her bedroom that everyone signed. And, much to her delight, she received a pair of pink tights from her mother. Sam was so happy she couldn't talk straight—and they all teased her good-naturedly about that.

Naomi laughed so hard about her near fall on examination day that she swallowed her gum, much to everyone's amusement. But of course she had several packs tucked in her jeans, so she passed them around, cheerfully grumbling about it.

But Lizinka shocked her. "What is this?" she asked solemnly.

"Why, it's gum!" Naomi said with a startled expression that made everyone burst into more laughter.

"What do you do with it? I've never had any before." Lizinka looked embarrassed.

"Chew it, of course!" Naomi's green eyes almost popped out of her head in amazement that anyone could not have been introduced to such an important part of her life. Her mouth formed a little round O, making her face look for all the world like an exclamation point.

Mrs. Scott, who was quietly listening, said, "Oh yes, I remember when Miss Jan came back from Russia, she told us about how the little boys would beg the tourists for 'goom'! You don't have any in your country, do you, Lizinka?"

"We could do without it here, too," Mr. Scott said under his breath to Aunt Emmy.

Then the cars began to come to pick up the girls, and one by one they started to leave, waving gaily as they went. Lizinka's car was the last to arrive. As she and Sam walked up to it, Lizinka reached her hand in her dress pocket and took out a small package.

"I did not have time to go to a department store," she said, "so I hope"— she searched for the words— "you will find it to your liking. It is mine, but I would like you to have it." Then, taking a deep breath, she said shyly, "This is the nicest time I have had since coming to America. Thank you, Sam." She said this softly, her blue eyes very serious.

Sam untied the pink ribbon and opened the little box. Nestled in a blue velvet case was a thin silver chain. As she lifted it out of the box, she saw a tiny, silver toe-shoe charm. It was so lovely it took her breath away.

"Ohhh, it's beautiful," sighed Sam, her breath catching in her throat.

"Thank you, Lee," she said before she suddenly remembered. Her eyes opened wide, and her hand went over her mouth. "Ooops, I'm *sorry*," she said emphatically. "I forgot. Honest! I mean—*Lizinka!*"

"No, do not apologize," Lizinka said, looking Sam right in the eye. "*I'm* sorry. I was rude that day. You see, I did not understand your American custom of shortening names. I thought you were making fun of me. I know now you were not. My father explained it to me. I wanted to tell you this before now, but the chance never seemed to come.

"It would make me very happy," Lizinka continued, her head lowered self-consciously, "if you would call me—Lee."

And without another word, she slipped into the waiting limousine and rode away.

6

En Pointe

It was early the next Monday morning. The sun was just peeking through Sam's bedroom window. A soft fall breeze blew the white organdy curtains, making them billow and fall with a rustle. Sam opened her eyes with a feeling of anticipation stirring in her body. Why was today special? Because this *was* a special day! She was certain of it. Then in a flash it came to her. Today she was going on toe for the very first time! This is what she had been working so hard for, the past three years. And now—she was ready.

It had been a wonderful week for Sam. Everything

was going her way. Being eleven years old was very exciting.

Mrs. Petrovna had phoned her mother and thanked her for her kindness to her daughter. Lizinka had told her about Sam and how she had misunderstood her attempts to be friends. Also, her grandmother, who had answered the phone, had thought a "dinner party" meant dressing up in party clothes. Sam had made Lizinka feel comfortable in spite of her incorrect attire. Mrs. Petrovna said that Sam must be a very sensitive and kind young lady.

Sam's mother had asked about the pendant. It was a lovely one, and she felt perhaps Lizinka had given it in desperation because she hadn't had a chance to go to a store. Mrs. Scott and Sam had talked about the possibility of returning it to Lizinka. Apparently, though, Lizinka had talked it over with her grandmother. The necklace was one Lizinka's father had given her when she first started taking ballet lessons, and Nanatasha said if she wanted Sam to have it, then of course she should give it to her.

So the necklace was Sam's as a bond of friendship. She reached up to her throat and felt the tiny silver chain and toe shoe so delicately made. Remembering the look on Lee's face as she had crouched in the corner of the limousine, Sam smiled to herself. How could she ever have misunderstood Lizinka? Why, she was no different from Sam! She had fears and worries too. Sam tried to imagine what it would be like to live in Russia. The thought was over-whelming!

Sam could hear the clatter of dishes in the kitchen and smell bacon frying. Her mother was making breakfast for her father. There was still a little time to daydream before school.

Jumping out of bed, she ran to her ballet box and for the umpteenth time took out her toe shoes. They had arrived in the mail two days before. She ran her fingers over the smooth pink satin. Miss Jan had warned them not to try to dance in them until she had explained the proper way. They might twist their ankles and not be able to dance at all, she had said.

Just slipping them on her foot couldn't do any harm, though. Sitting on the floor, she slid a foot into each slipper and stretched her legs out straight in front of her, arching her toes into a lovely sharp point. They were so beautiful, and today she would be dancing in them! Miss Jan had said it would not be easy, but she was sure she could do it.

"Sam!" called her mother from the foot of the stairs. "Are you up? It's getting late."

Quickly she put her toe shoes in the ballet box, gave her new pink tights a special pat, and got ready for school.

At ballet class Sam felt very elegant in her black leotard and pink tights. She glanced over at Lizinka, who was dressed the same way. They smiled shyly at one another as they walked across the studio floor with the rest of the girls. Each girl was carrying her toe shoes and trying to appear casual.

"Sit on the benches, class," Miss Jan said with a big smile. "You must learn how to put on your toe shoes properly.

"There is no right or left to a toe shoe, girls, so it doesn't matter which foot you put the slipper on."

The class knew this from wearing ballet slippers, so it came as no surprise.

"Now, put your lamb's-wool toe pad over your toes. Later you may find you prefer the loose lamb's wool, so you can place it in strategic spots as you need it. For now, though, this is easier to handle.

"Slide your foot into the slipper and place the tip of the toe on the floor, wriggling your foot into it until it feels right." The class did as they were told in breathless anticipation.

"With the toe pointed, cross the satin ribbons over the front of the ankle once," she continued. "Be sure that the ribbon is straight and smooth, or it will cut into your leg. Then bring both ribbons around to the back and over the front and to the inside ankle. Have you got it?"

Everyone did as she was told.

"Fine, class. Beautiful! Now tie a knot at the ankle, and all that extra ribbon will be cut off."

"I thought you tied a bow," said Michelle.

"No, never! Always a neat knot, with the ends tucked away to give a smooth look and so you won't

trip over them. Now, if you're ready, we will go over to the *barre* and give them a try."

They all stood up and walked self-consciously to the *barre*. Their shoes were stiff and made a clackety sound as the girls walked across the floor.

"Face the *barre*, class. Hold on lightly with *both* hands. Feet together. Now, pull up through the half toe—be sure to *bend* your toe shoe at this point. Then on up to the full point. Hold it," she said. There were a few groans. "And down the same way. Don't forget to break at the half toe."

Miss Jan put the music on and counted, *"Relevé,* two three four, five six seven eight. Lower, two three four, five six seven eight. Straighten the knees. We can't have knobby knees. Relax the shoulders."

The class worked intensely for ten minutes. But oh, how it hurts, thought Sam. This wasn't exactly what she had thought it would be like.

"When your shoes are broken in, you will find it much easier to move in them, girls. Don't be discouraged. You're doing fine. I said it would be hard, remember?"

"Yes, but not *this* hard!" said Michelle with a discouraged look.

"All right," said Miss Jan, sensing that they had had enough for the first time. "Take off your toe shoes now."

Twelve girls, limping and groaning, sat on the floor and took off their toe shoes.

"Ooohhh—aaaahhh—that feels good!" they exclaimed, wriggling their toes and rubbing them deliciously.

"I'll never be able to do it," said Lisa.

"Oh yes, you will, dear," said Miss Jan. "Wait and see. Practice in your toe shoes ten minutes each day for the first week. Now, ready for your *révérence*."

To the strains of the *Sleeping Beauty* Waltz, they all bowed to their teacher. Dance class was over. For the first time, the girls seemed a bit discouraged.

Starting for the dressing room, Lizinka passed Sam, and she smiled and said, "My toes are tingling. Are yours?"

"Mm-hmm." Sam nodded, rolling her eyes wide. They both laughed, and Lizinka, noticing that her car had arrived, said, "See you next week, Sam," and hurried to the waiting car.

7

Miss Jan Plans a Recital

Sure enough, as the weeks went by, the girls got up on their toes for longer periods and began to get into the center and do little steps—even little toe dances. Now it started to be fun.

Sam would often turn on her record player at home, put on her toe shoes, and practice. But she never got around to practicing every single day, as Miss Jan had told them to. She knew that her friends did not practice every day, either. None of them, that is, except Lizinka.

Sam's intentions were good, but something would

always crop up to change her plans. There would be a television show she didn't want to miss, or she'd start reading a good book and wouldn't be able to put it down. But as production planning time drew near, Sam knew that she had to start practicing every day or she would not get a part in the recital. Each year Miss Jan would choose the cast from her advanced students and from the younger ones who danced especially well. Last year Sam had been one of the Royal Children in scenes from *Sleeping Beauty*. It was fun because they were on stage several times and had to act as well as dance. Sam was good at this because she loved to pretend. The girls were eagerly waiting to hear what this year's story would be about.

As they walked into class the Monday before Christmas vacation, Miss Jan had costume books in her hand and looked very excited. Just before class ended, she told them to sit down because she had some interesting news to tell them.

"This year," she said, "we are going to do a real ballet. It will be the students' version of *The Nutcracker*. If you sit quietly, I'll tell you the story."

"Oh, good! We will, Miss Jan," the girls said, settling themselves down on the floor.

"Well," Miss Jan said, "this ballet is generally done at Christmastime, but this is the first year I've had enough students in my classes to attempt it. It has great parts for children your age and is such a delightful story that I am certain we'll be forgiven for performing it a few months out of season.

"The year is 1892 in the country of Germany. The first act opens on a beautiful scene in the living room of the Governor and his wife. A huge Christmas tree is ablaze with lights, and the room is decorated with boughs and holly. They are having an old-fashioned Christmas party, and the guests begin to arrive. The ladies are dressed in beautiful gowns and diamond jewelry; the gentlemen are handsome figures in their tuxedos. Clara and Franz, the Governor's children, join the festivities dressed in their holiday clothes. Franz wears black velvet knee pants, a white ruffled shirt, and knee socks; Clara wears a red velvet dress with white lace. Other children arrive with their parents, and it is a very happy time.

"Uncle Drosselmeyer, a very strange and funny character, arrives with gifts for all the children— especially a pretty, hand-carved nutcracker for his favorite niece, Clara. Franz is jealous of his sister's gift, and there is a squabble. Franz breaks the nutcracker, and Clara bursts into tears. She stops crying when Uncle Drosselmeyer bandages the broken toy and asks her to put it to bed in a cradle under the Christmas tree. Refreshments are served. The grown-ups perform the Grandfather Dance with the children, ending the party. Everyone leaves."

"I went to New York to see it last year with my mom and dad," Naomi boasted.

"So did I," Michelle said.

"It sounds beautiful," said Samantha.

"It *is* beautiful." Lizinka surprised everyone by chiming in enthusiastically. "I saw the ballet in Moscow. The music is by Tchaikovsky. He's Russian, you know," she said proudly.

"I know, Lizinka," Miss Jan answered. "Perhaps you'd like to tell us the rest of the story."

"Well," Lizinka said, completely forgetting her shyness in her enthusiasm, "after everyone goes to bed, Clara comes back into the living room to see the broken nutcracker. Only the Christmas-tree lights are on, and the stage looks beautiful."

"Is Clara in her nightgown when she comes in?" asked Lisa.

"Yes," Miss Jan replied, "she is. And she falls asleep in the big easy chair by the Christmas tree, holding the bandaged nutcracker."

"Then a wondrous thing happens," continued Lizinka in very proper English with just a trace of accent. "The nutcracker turns into a handsome prince!

"The prince leads Clara to the Land of Snow— where the beautiful Snow Queen makes the Snowflakes lie down, and Clara dances among them. Then they take Clara to the Kingdom of Sweets."

"And there they meet the lovely Sugar Plum Fairy, who welcomes them, and they hold a festival for Clara," Miss Jan went on.

"I saw Nadezhda Pavlova dance in *The Nutcracker*," said Lizinka. "I even saw her rehearse." She was so excited she couldn't stop talking.

"How wonderful, Lizinka! You're a lucky girl to have had the opportunity," their teacher said, smiling warmly at her.

"Yes, I've only seen one real ballet," said Sam sadly. "Lucky you," she said, looking at Lizinka enviously.

"Oh, I've been to lots of them," she said, with a slight toss of her head.

"In the next act there are what we call Character Dances, which are Russian, Chinese, Arabian, and others. The ballet ends with everyone taking part in the grand finale."

"What parts will we play in the ballet, Miss Jan?" asked the girls eagerly.

"Well, this is the very exciting part of it all. This class is just the right age to be the children at the party, and someone here will play Clara, the lead. . . ."

The girls looked wide-eyed at their teacher, mouths open, hardly daring to breathe.

"Who is it? Who is it? Oh, I hope it's me!" each girl squealed. Sam's heart beat fast. How she would love to be Clara! She would work so hard—if only she could be. Glancing over at Lizinka, she was surprised to see wide-eyed longing in her eyes also. She wanted the part too! Before Lizinka had come, the choice from this class would have been a sure thing. Everyone had agreed Sam was the best dancer. Now—well, now it was a different story. Now she was second best. Why did Lizinka have to join *this* class, anyway? Sam thought, pouting.

Laughing at the girls, Miss Jan said, "You will all have good parts, you'll see. I'll see you all after Christmas and I'll tell you what parts you will play at that time.

"Stand for the *grande révérence*, class."

Getting into place, they all made their bows to Miss Jan.

"Merry Christmas, all." She smiled.

"Merry Christmas, Miss Jan," they chorused as they left the studio.

A Visit to Lizinka's

Christmas week at Sam's house was very exciting. There was no school and no dance class, but there were lots and lots of things to do. There was good food to prepare, presents to buy and wrap, her Sunday-school party to go to, and Christmas caroling for the senior citizens and shut-ins. And, of course, the most fun of all was putting up the Christmas tree. It made Sam think of *The Nutcracker*. Her parents had some friends and relatives in: Aunt Em and Uncle Charlie and AnneMarie and little Emily. The grown-ups talked and the children exchanged gifts and made popcorn. Her older cousins, Cathy, Robyn, Denice, and Kara, came, as well as her favorite young cousins, Christopher Nathan, and Amos Tobias.

That night Sam went to bed bursting with happiness. She was hoping for a new pair of figure skates because the town had built a large skating rink on the Common. It even had lights for night skating! Her mother had said this year she could go up after supper on weekends to skate until eight o'clock. Some of her friends were hoping for skates, too, and Sam knew she would enjoy having them because dancing and figure skating were so much alike. But much as she wanted the skates, there was something she longed for even more.

Kneeling at her bed, eyes closed tightly and hands folded for prayer, Sam let her mind race around for a while and then quiet down.

"Dear God," she whispered softly, "I know I'm so lucky to have such a nice home and such a nice mom and dad. . . ."

She paused and thought about it for a while. She *was* lucky, she knew it, and she also knew very well that she shouldn't bargain with God. But this meant so much to her, she just couldn't help herself.

"Dear God," Sam continued, "if I could be Clara in *The Nutcracker*, I wouldn't wish for skates or anything else in the world. I would work *so* hard. I'd make Miss Jan proud she chose me." Her eyes clouded with tears; her chin trembled in spite of herself.

After a few minutes, Sam stood up and got into bed. She stretched out straight in her bed, hands behind her head, and thought about it. She envisioned Clara in her red velvet party dress; Clara after the party, coming into the living room, sitting in the big easy chair by the soft glow of the Christmas-tree lights; the appearance of the Prince and how he would lead her into the Land of Ice and Snow; and Clara dancing—maybe on toe!—among the Snow-flakes! The visions her mind created were so lovely, they took her breath away. . . .

The next thing she knew, her mother was calling. It was morning.

"Samantha," her mother said, "you're wanted on the telephone."

Rubbing her eyes, she ran down the stairs and wondered who could be calling her.

"Hi," she said sleepily into the phone.

"Hello, Sam," an unfamiliar voice answered. "This is Lee."

"Oh, hi," answered Sam with a surprised giggle.

"Could you come over for luncheon today, Sam? My mamma and pappa have gone to New York. Nanatasha said I could ask you. I hope you can come, Sam." It was a lonely little voice, and for a reason that she couldn't explain, Sam felt sorry for her.

Her mother was in the same room, so, putting her hand over the mouthpiece, Sam whispered, "It's

A Visit to Lizinka's

Lizinka, Mom. She wants me to come to lunch. May
I, please?"

"But, honey, I thought you were looking forward
to making cookies today," her mother said.

"I can do that tomorrow, Mom. Please?" she
pleaded.

"Well, I guess it's all right if you really want to,"
her mother said. "Find out what time, and I'll drive
you over."

Into the phone Sam said happily, "When shall I
come, Lee? Mom will drive me over."

"As soon as you can," Lizinka answered.

Just as Sam and her mother were leaving, the
phone rang again. This time it *was* Naomi.

"Can I come over and bake cookies with you
today?" she asked enthusiastically. "Mom has to go
Christmas shopping, and I don't want to go."

"Oh, Naomi, I'm sorry. I just promised Lizinka I'd
go over there," Sam answered.

"Where?!" Naomi asked. "You gotta be kidding!
What will you do over there? Watch her dance?"

"She just asked me to lunch," Sam said, ignoring
the sarcastic remark. "Her folks are away, and I think
she's lonesome."

"She's weird, Sam! Michelle thinks so, too. Did
you see her give your mother those silly wild
flowers? You can pick them anywhere in the
meadows, for gosh sakes, and she handed them to
her upside down—dumb!"

"Well, yeah," Sam reluctantly admitted, "it did look kind of funny. Maybe she just was so nervous she didn't know what she was doing."

"Oh *sure* she was!" Sam heard a little snap and knew that Naomi was popping her gum to emphasize her point. "See you around," said Naomi, and she slammed the receiver down so hard it stung Sam's ears.

Lee lived about ten minutes out of town in a secluded old country house. To get to it one had to go through a huge gate and down what seemed like miles of winding driveway, past tall poplar trees on either side. As they drove up, Sam could see Lizinka waiting at the picture window. It wasn't even five seconds before the big front door burst open and Lizinka came running out to their car, pigtails flying. A heavy-set woman in a pretty blue wool dress, with silver-gray hair pulled straight back in a low bun, stood in the doorway. "That must be Nanatasha," thought Sam.

"Hello, Lizinka," Sam's mother said. "You two should have a lot to talk about so close to Christmas. What time shall I pick Sam up?"

"Boris has to go to town later this afternoon. He will drive Sam home, Mrs. Scott, if it is all right with you," said Lizinka.

"Oh, that will be fine," Mrs. Scott said. "Have fun, girls." With a smile and a wave of her hand, she drove off.

A Visit to Lizinka's

Taking Sam's hand, Lee pulled her toward the house. When she reached the woman in blue, Lizinka quieted down noticeably.

"This is Samantha, Nanatasha," she said primly. "Samantha, this is my grandmamma."

Sam had a feeling that she was expected to curtsy. But she looked up into the face of the Russian woman and saw kind, blue eyes and a sweet smile. Nanatasha reached out her hand and patted Sam's head.

"I hear many nice things about you, Samantha," said Nanatasha pleasantly. "I am—glad—to meet you." Her words came out slowly and distinctly, after much thought, and Sam realized English was strange to her. But what she couldn't say with words Nanatasha said with her eyes, and Samantha felt the warmth of her welcome.

"Come! See our Christmas tree, Sam!" Lizinka said, grabbing her hand and pulling her into the house. "Nanatasha is making pancakes for our luncheon and will call us when they are ready."

When they got to the large family room, they found a friendly fire crackling in the fireplace and a huge tree decorated in the middle of the room. Sam had never seen one placed that way, and it looked pretty sitting there. Their own tree at home was always put in a corner or by a window.

"It's beautiful," she said, and as they sat on the rug by the fireplace she asked, "What are you hoping to get this Christmas?"

"Oh, I don't know." Lizinka laughed. "You see, we do not celebrate Christmas in Russia as you do here. The holiday we celebrate is on the New Year. Then we have family and friends come to the house, and we have a feast and sing songs and dance. We also exchange little gifts. Our Christmas is on January sixth, and is very solemn. We have a Christmas tree here now because we like to follow the custom of the country in which we are living."

"Oh, really?" Sam was amazed. "I would miss celebrating Christmas!"

"Do *you* have a special wish for Christmas?" Lizinka asked.

"Oh, I don't know—I'd like skates," Sam answered, not wanting to admit to Lizinka her *real* wish of the night before. "We have a new skating rink in town with lights for night skating. Do you like to skate?"

"Oh yes, we do lots of skating in Moscow. Every little park has a skating pond. I love it when I have time for it. But I am very busy at school and my ballet. We have a little pond here beside the house. Why don't I see if we can have a skating party sometime soon?"

"That would be super," Sam said. "That would be neat, to skate on your own pond." Then, because she sensed Lee's need to talk about her family, Sam asked, "Will your mom and dad be gone long?"

"Oh, they will be back here by the holidays," she

answered, assuming a matter-of-fact air. "You see, Pappa has certain diplomatic duties to attend to. Mamma has to go along, too, at this time of the year."

"I'd be lonesome if my mom and dad had to be away during the Christmas season," Sam said seriously. She felt bad for her friend.

"I get used to it. Last year they were in Japan. I was really lonely then. I stayed home with Nanatasha. This time we all wanted to be together, so the state arranged it for us. It's not so bad when Nanatasha is with me, but I do miss my school friends."

"Where do you go to school now?" asked Sam, suddenly realizing that she had not seen Lizinka at their school.

"Oh, Boris is my private tutor. He is a university graduate and is traveling with us this year. He acts as a chauffeur also. Our classes are quite different from yours. You see, we go to school year round. In the summer we go off to camp."

"Oh, wow! School year round! I wouldn't like that! I like to go to the ocean in the summer." Sam was horrified.

Lizinka, seeing Sam flustered over the thought of going to school all summer, burst into laughter. Sam, seeing her new friend so happy, joined in the laughter, and they both tumbled over backward in a fit of giggling. Any strangeness they had felt about each other disappeared.

Nanatasha, standing in the doorway, watched

them with a look of contentment on her face. Lizinka was happy, so she was happy too.

"Luncheon it is ready, little ones," she called.

Faces flushed with laughter, the girls stood up, straightened their skirts, and ran to the dining room.

The table was like a picture in a magazine, Sam thought. The tablecloth was dark green, and the dishes were sparkling white with a gold band around the edge. In the center of the table was a bowl of red cherries with a tapered candle in the middle.

An unfamiliar aroma reached Sam's hungry nose. What was placed before her didn't look like a pancake as she knew it.

Noticing Sam's puzzled expression, Lizinka asked, "Haven't you ever had *blinis*?"

"Bleen-us?" echoed Sam like a parrot.

Laughing again, Lizinka explained.

"They are potato pancakes. Nanatasha makes mine very thin with crisp brown lace edges because she knows I like them that way." Scooping some sour cream from a bowl, she firmly plopped a generous spoonful over the little flat pancake. Cutting a piece with her fork, she popped it into her mouth. "MMMM-Hmmm!" Lizinka said and closed her eyes for an instant to get the full flavor with no interference from outside. "I *love* them! I have not had any since leaving Moscow."

Gingerly Sam followed suit, trying not to appear rude by hesitating. She chewed thoughtfully for a few seconds, then beamed and rolled her eyes appreciatively. "They *are* good! Really tasty! I hope I can get the recipe so Mom can make them sometime."

"Of course. Grandmamma will give it to you, I'm sure," Lizinka said, pleased.

"Do you like buttermilk, Samantha?" Nanatasha asked, pouring a glass for Lizinka.

"Oh yes, thank you, I do!" Sam said, although she seldom had it at home.

"Here's the sugar and jam, Sam," Lizinka said, passing her a little silver tray.

This time Sam was thoroughly baffled. She felt as if she had stepped into another world—it was all so different.

"Don't you like sugar and jam in your buttermilk? See, I'll show you." And Lizinka scooped two generous teaspoons of sugar into her glass of buttermilk along with a spoonful of jam—stirring it all vigorously with a spoon.

Wait until I tell Naomi about this, thought Sam. She'll really flip out.

After lunch was over, the girls helped Nanatasha clear the table. Just as they were finishing up, who should walk into the kitchen but Boris, holding a small bunch of flowers *upside down!* By this time Sam thought she must be through the looking glass with Alice, so bewildered was she. Without thinking, she said, "Why are you holding those flowers that way?"

"What way?" Boris asked. His eyes twinkled.

"Upside down!" pursued Sam boldly. She just *had* to know so she could tell Naomi about it.

"Oh, that!" Boris answered, laughing. He was a handsome young man. "Why, it's so the juices don't flow out," he explained. "They last longer that way."

"Really?" There was no end to the things she was learning.

"Yes," Boris continued. He seemed anxious to talk. "We Russians love flowers. I don't see too many people carrying them in America. We pick them or buy them every day and take them to one another wherever we go. Even the bus drivers have a little fresh bouquet daily beside them on the sills of their windows. There is a hothouse on the grounds and a gardener who tends to the flowers all year round. He lets me pick some whenever I want. These," he said, holding them out to Sam, "are for my limousine."

Sam and Lee went back into the living room and sat down on the rug by the fireplace once more. They had learned so much about one another this day. They had not, however, talked about the thing closest to both their hearts—their dancing.

They were silent for a moment, looking into the fire, each with her own thoughts, when Lizinka said, "Do you want to be a ballerina, Samantha?"

"I don't know," Sam said uncertainly. "I'd *like* to. But I'm not sure I'm good enough." Then: "Would you?"

"I'm *going* to be a ballerina," Lizinka said flatly. Looking squarely at Sam, she added, "Nothing can stop me."

Lizinka's firmness stunned Samantha, who had never seriously thought about being grown up. She now looked upon her determined Russian friend with new respect. But they did not discuss their ambitions anymore that day.

The afternoon flew by, and before they knew it, Nanatasha was smiling kindly in the doorway and saying that Boris was ready to go into town. Sam got up reluctantly; then impulsively she ran up to Lizinka's grandmother and put her arms around her broad waist. Giving her a squeeze, she said, "Thank you for a lovely lunch, Nanatasha."

"We are very happy to have you, Samantha. I hope you will come again," she answered.

As she stepped out the big front door, Sam saw Boris standing by the door of the limousine. When the girls approached, he opened the door with a flourish and, holding Sam gently by the elbow, helped her step into the big car. As it moved slowly away from the big house, Samantha waved her hand to Lizinka and her grandmother, who stood holding hands at the big front door.

As the car rolled smoothly along the winding driveway, Samantha had the feeling that she was a princess. A glass partition separated her from the chauffeur in the front seat, and she let her imagination run wild. It seemed like a fantasy land.

Raising her hand in a regal gesture and nodding her head with great dignity, first right then left, she imagined that she was bowing to her loyal subjects. Suddenly she caught the twinkling eyes of Boris watching her in the car mirror. Embarrassed, she slouched deep into the cushions of the big car seat and wished she could vanish from sight.

Before long she was home. Hoping to skip away without having to say anything to Boris, she reached for the car door, but Boris was too quick for her. As he opened the door for Samantha, he made an elaborate bow from the waist and said, "The Royal Palace, Princess Samantha!" and helped her out. Keeping her head lowered, she quickly slipped by him, but as she got up to her gate, she couldn't resist glancing back. Boris stood looking after her, and when she turned, he winked broadly and grinned.

Giggling, Samantha skipped into the house to tell her mother about her exciting day.

Clara is Chosen

Sam's feet hardly touched the stairs on Christmas morning. Her heart skipped as she ran into the living room to look at her gifts. She had been working very hard on an embroidered cross-stitch picture for her mother, and she had knitted a navy-blue scarf for her dad, and she was anxious to see if they liked them. Of course they did! And they couldn't imagine how she had found time to do it without being seen.

"Oh, I kept them at school and worked during recess," Sam explained, her eyes shining.

Sure enough, nestled in the branches of the

beautiful tree was a pair of figure skates trimmed with white fur! Sam brushed the soft fur across her cheeks, filled with happiness. She would go skating that very afternoon. And she would call Naomi to see if she could go with her.

Sam pushed aside the still-nagging desire to play the part of Clara in *The Nutcracker*. Her desire was still very much there, but there was nothing she could do about it. She had received the skates, so she decided to enjoy them. And enjoy them she did! Skating was so much like ballet, and Sam's body was strong and coordinated.

All the girls met at the Common that afternoon. Sam was surprised to see Naomi had new skates too. The girls tried *arabesques* on skates, throwing their heads back and balancing on one leg with the brisk wind biting their cheeks. They laughed hysterically when they bumped into one another and landed not so gracefully on their derrieres.

It was a happy week, full of exciting things. Sam loved her book about ballet, with its beautifully colored pictures of different scenes. She looked long and hard at the one from *The Nutcracker*. Clara was so beautiful. The snow scene was lovely too. Even being a guest at the Christmas party was not something to be sneezed at.

The Saturday morning before vacation was to end, Sam received a phone call from Lizinka. Nanatasha had said she could have a skating party at her home!

The pond behind her house was like glass and just perfect for skating. Nanatasha had suggested she invite a few girls over. Since Lizinka didn't know their last names, she asked Sam if she would be willing to call them for her.

"Sounds super," said Sam. "Tell me who to call. What time shall we come? I'm sure Mom will take us. I'll call you in an hour."

After they hung up, Sam ran to ask her if she could go.

"I think it would be lots of fun," said Mrs. Scott. "What a nice way to wind up your Christmas vacation! Have the girls come over here, and I'll drive you to Lizinka's house."

So Samantha got busy on the phone. They were to meet at her house at a quarter to two and they would be back before dark, which would be by four-thirty. The girls all thought it would be great fun and said they would be at Sam's house right on time.

Adorned in new Christmas hats and scarves, skates slung over their shoulders, they gathered in Sam's kitchen. There were Michelle and Lisa, Debbie, Evie, and of course Naomi.

"Let's go, girls," Sam's mother said. Chattering like monkeys, they all piled into the station wagon.

"Where does Lizinka live, anyway?" asked Evie.

"It's out of town about five miles," replied Sam importantly. After all she had been there before, and having to invite the girls for Lizinka made her feel almost like a co-hostess. "Do you know the place they call the Fox Mansion? It used to belong to Senator Fox. Well, that's where she lives."

"You mean that place that looks like an old castle, with a long, long driveway and poplar trees on both sides?" asked Michelle excitedly.

"That's the one," Sam answered, very pleased to be so in the know.

"Wow!"

"Hey, great!"

"I've never been there."

"We went up the driveway once when it was vacant, just to see the pretty flowers. They have a gardener who lives there year round."

When Mrs. Scott turned off the main road and started up the driveway to the old Fox Mansion, the girls immediately became quiet.

A light snow had fallen, and the trees sparkled in the sunshine. The house had tall pillars and a white front door decorated with a huge wreath tied with a big red bow. It did indeed look like a picture-book castle.

As the car stopped and the girls piled out, they looked to Sam to lead the way. Then in the clear, cold air they heard a voice calling, "Over here, Sam! Come on over!"

Across a stretch of lawn, and what would have been a garden had it been summer, was a small pond shimmering in the sunshine. A girl in a bright red coat with a white fur hat and muff stood at the pond, waving excitedly, beckoning them to join her.

"Let's go," said Sam, and off they went, trying to outrun each other, laughing and panting breathlessly as they reached the pond.

"I'm glad you could all come," Lizinka said, smiling shyly, looking from one to another. "You can put on your skates in the grape arbor over there, if you'd like, or here on the bench. It was such a perfect day I didn't want to waste a minute of it, so I didn't wait. Hope you don't mind."

"Of course not!" they answered, almost in unison. "We'll be with you in a minute." And off they went to change. Sam and Naomi sat on the nearby bench and quickly pulled off their boots and started putting on their skates.

Lizinka pushed off gracefully into a backward twist and went into a figure eight, her graceful body strong and sure.

Sam, still lacing her skates, felt a pang of envy as she watched her friend. Is there anything she can't do? she thought. Then she deliberately pushed the thought out of her mind. "I mustn't," she said to herself. "I like Lizinka, I really do, but must she be so good at everything?"

Soon the pond was a blaze of color as the girls started weaving in and out on the ice. They all skated fairly well, but Lizinka outshone everyone. So they began asking her help with their own moves, and she taught the other girls games that relaxed them. Soon they all lost their stiffness and found themselves feeling completely at home on their skates. One maneuver left them breathless and down in a heap, laughing hysterically.

The time slipped by like quicksilver, and soon they heard the tinkling of a bell. Looking in the direction of the house, Lizinka could see her grandmother standing in the doorway.

"We've got to go in now, girls," she said. "It must be getting late."

Quickly the girls took off their skates. They headed for the house with cold cheeks and smelling of fresh clean air. As they entered the front door, a delicious aroma greeted their red noses.

"Come in, come in, young ladies," said Nanatasha, smiling. "It's nice to see you again, Samantha," she added, giving her head a gentle pat.

On the table was a board with hot slices of bread, golden butter, raspberry jam, and a pitcher of steaming hot chocolate.

The girls did not need any coaxing, as the fresh air had made them hungry. The hot bread, fresh out of the oven, was so delicious with the melted butter and jam that it disappeared like magic. But as the girls sipped the cocoa, a strange expression came over their faces.

"What's the matter?" asked Lizinka. "Is something wrong?"

"Not wrong! Just different," volunteered Lisa. "The cocoa tastes—uh—strange."

"Oh, I know why." Lizinka laughed. "It's Russian chocolate. It has a bit of coffee in it and a touch of mint."

"You sure do have some delicious foods," said Sam, feeling like a connoisseur of foreign dishes. After all, she had had *blinis*, and buttermilk a new way too.

On the way home that afternoon, they all agreed it had been fun. "She's not a bad kid when you get to know her," even Naomi admitted reluctantly.

That evening Sam took a hot bath and cuddled up in her warm flannel nightgown. She read a chapter of her new ballet book, and the book was hardly closed and the light out before she was fast asleep.

Vacation was over now and Christmas behind them. It had been a lovely time for Samantha and her friends.

"Welcome back, class," said Miss Jan with a smile. "Now that the holidays are over, I hope you are all ready to settle down to some real hard work."

There was a tenseness in the air, a realization that today they would be assigned their special parts in *The Nutcracker*.

"Class will break five minutes early," Miss Jan continued, "so that I can tell you more about our recital plans. Right now, let's get to the *barre* and try

(92)

to pull ourselves back into shape. I'm sure we've all indulged in too much good food and lazy habits."

Smiling sheepishly and nodding in agreement, the class assembled at the *barre* and started their *pliés*. As they progressed from one exercise to another, here and there a muffled groan could be heard when an exercise put demands on their muscles.

Samantha felt a happy tingle as she bent and stretched with all her might, trying to push all thoughts of the recital out of her mind. She had taken special care to pull her hair up in a knot off her neck. But as she exercised, a few short tendrils escaped from her upswept hair and hung in springy little wisps around her face. It was nice to be dancing again. She felt a kinship to all the people in this classroom who shared the love of dance with her. Glancing at Lizinka, she felt a common bond that even the width of an ocean could not separate.

So absorbed was she in her own thoughts that she was startled to hear Miss Jan's voice call out, "Center floor, please, class. Take a partner; dancers to right face upstage, and dancers to left face downstage." Before Samantha could collect her thoughts, she found Lizinka beside her, a tentative smile on her face. Her solemn blue eyes questioned Samantha.

"Be my partner, Sam?" Lizinka asked softly. Looking back with a slight toss of her head, Sam nodded lightly. Observing Sam, one would never guess she was almost bursting with pride.

Positioning themselves on the floor, they waited for instructions from their teacher. There was some scuffling and giggling over choosing partners. Miss Jan waited patiently; then she said:

"Starting with the right foot and working back to back with your partner, do *balancé, balancé soutenu,* turn, three times. All will finish to front on third turn. *Arabesque* right; step left, and *tendu* right back. Then *port de bras.* Let's all mark it before trying it to music."

Samantha looked at Lizinka, eyebrows raised. She thought she understood the combination, but for some unknown reason she held back. Usually Sam plunged into her dance steps with great confidence, but Lizinka's presence made her reluctant to do it, for fear of making a mistake. Glancing at Lizinka, she could sense her assurance, and with it her own confidence returned.

"And a . . . *balancé, balancé soutenu,* turn, and one two three, one two three, one two three four five six. *Balancé, balancé soutenu,* turn, to the front. *Arabesque* two three, step two three. *Port de bras* two three four five six."

There was a little fumbling here and there, and questions about positioning of arms by some, and then a quieting down and feeling of readiness to try again.

"And . . . a . . . *balancé, balancé soutenu,* turn," Miss Jan continued on through the combination again. This time it went more smoothly and picked up speed. Another time through and they were ready for the music.

Sam's eyes shone as she listened to the delightful waltz melody. It sounded familiar to her, yet she couldn't actually name it.

"You are dancing to the music from *The Nutcracker*," Miss Jan explained. "Isn't it beautiful? It's the 'Waltz of the Flowers'—are we ready to try our combination to it?"

Going to the record player, she started the music again, counting through the introduction, leading them into the steps.

Samantha lost herself in the movement of the dance, enjoying it so completely that she felt a twinge of sadness when it was over. She was pulled back to reality when Miss Jan said, "Very good, class. Now please sit down so I can talk to you about your recital parts."

A hush came over the studio. As Samantha sat down, she again found herself next to Lizinka. She was afraid the class could hear her heart pounding in her breast.

"I've given a great deal of thought to casting in this ballet, because of course we want it to be very good. First of all, let me say that all of you, except the one who plays the part of Clara, will be dancing to the 'Waltz of the Flowers.' You have been doing so well on toe—or to be correct, I should say *en pointe*," she said smiling, "that you have just learned one of the

combinations in your recital dance in class today!"

"Really? That was fun. What do we wear?" Words tumbled over one another in the girls excitement.

"Each one of you will be able to choose your favorite color," their teacher said. "Your costume will be a classic *tutu*, and you'll wear a garland of flowers in your hair. It will be very elegant." Miss Jan paused, looking first at one and then another.

"However, it means a lot of hard work, as you must dance with a teen-age girl who will be playing the Queen of the Flowers. You are her *corps de ballet*. Do you think you can handle it?" Miss Jan asked this seriously.

Their sparkling eyes made it clear that they were very pleased.

"Now," Miss Jan continued, taking a deep breath, "I've had to cast four of you in the first act as guests of the Governor and his wife—the little cousins who come to the Christmas party with their parents, remember? I couldn't choose all of you, as it would overcrowd the stage. Since I'd like an even number of boys and girls, and since the boys in the dance class are not too tall, I decided to choose the shortest girls in this class for the young guests. Any one of you would be capable of playing the part, as it calls for more acting than dancing."

"Who is Clara?" they burst out almost in unison. "You said she'd be from this class!"

"So I did, so I did!" She laughed. "I thought I'd

wait to tell you that news last, but since you all are so impatient, I won't keep you in suspense any longer. It was a very difficult decision, and I thought long and hard before making a choice. . . ."

Samantha closed her eyes for an instant and said a little prayer.

Her hands were clasped tightly in her lap. Opening her eyes, she could see Miss Jan talking, but the voice seemed to drone on and on from a great distance. The words had no meaning. She leaned forward and held her breath to stop the pounding in her head, just as the words "Lizinka for the part of Clara" reached her ears.

She heard the class react with excitement and she saw the look of pure joy come over Lizinka's face. Samantha's face felt like a mask. She blinked fast to keep the tears back and felt her lips stretch into a stiff little smile.

"Debby, Michelle, Naomi, and Samantha will be the little cousins," Miss Jan finished, then said, "Ready for your *révérence,* class." Everyone stood to get into place for her final bow. Samantha took this time to regain her composure and hide her disappointment.

As the class ended, some of the girls gathered around Lizinka, congratulating her. Some talked about their "Waltz of the Flowers," others about their parts as young guests.

Only alert Naomi sensed Sam's misery. "You

should have the lead, Sam," she whispered in her ear as she squeezed Sam hard around the neck.

Trying to keep the disappointment out of her face, Sam moved toward Lizinka. Her voice sounded shrill to her own ears, but she smiled brightly as she congratulated Lee on being picked for the part of Clara.

"I'm glad we're in Act One together," Lizinka said. Nodding quickly, Samantha gathered her clothes in a little bundle as if in a hurry and quickly stepped out of the studio.

Walking briskly toward home, she was thankful that it was a little dusky, for she could no longer hold back the tears that stung her eyes and rolled down her cheeks.

"I must be a good sport," she scolded herself. "Lizinka deserved the part."

As she rounded the corner to her home, a sob escaped. How could she tell her mother about this? She bit her lip hard to keep back the tears. Entering the kitchen, she saw her mother talking on the phone. Mrs. Scott's smile of welcome changed to one of concern when she saw Sam's face.

"Are you all right, Sam, dear?" she asked with a worried look, holding her hand over the mouthpiece.

"I've got a little stomachache," Sam answered, holding her hand over her stomach and smiling weakly at her mother. "Think I'll just go to bed," she said, heading for her room.

She lay on her back. The pillow felt cool and smooth on her hot cheek, and the darkness enveloped her so that she felt safe from prying eyes. No need to hide her disappointment now. No need to pretend anymore. Not until she had wept long and hard and found herself completely drained of all emotion did she hear a gentle knock on her door.

"May I come in, Sam?" her mother asked, pushing the door open softly as she said it. She felt her mother's comforting arms around her. Her mother knew. There was no need for words. No need for explaining. She understood.

10

Challenge and Celebration

The winter months were cold and long, but for Samantha the days flew by. There was schoolwork, of course, but most of that was done in the classroom. Luckily Samantha's teacher felt that children should not be burdened with too much homework. Her friends took their skates to school and they all gathered on the Common for a few whirls after class. By four-thirty it was dark, so Samantha had to head for home. She liked to help her mother set the table, and she loved making the salad so much that it became her self-appointed chore. Then she put on her ballet record and faithfully went through her *barre* work. She had set herself the goal of improving her extension. Lizinka was able to raise her leg so high that it was the envy of all the class.

Ballet became more and more an important part of Sam's life, and observing Lizinka, she began to realize it was a jealous art, demanding dedication and hard work. With the young Prince in *The Nutcracker*, Lizinka had begun to practice her *pas de deux*, which in the language of ballet means "dance for two." Sam watched Lizinka bend and stretch her body to the fullest, stoically putting demands on it until beads of perspiration glistened on her forehead. She realized that she had never really worked very hard. In the past when she had become tired, she had quit. More and more now she made herself stretch her body until she became aware of each muscle and felt it tingle. She actually began to enjoy the feeling of being physically exhausted—looking forward to her hot bubble bath and cozy flannel nightgown after her one-and-a-half-hour exercise session.

As the weeks went by, she became aware of the appreciative glances of her ballet class when she extended her leg at the *barre,* stretched it high above her waist, and held it there. She accepted their appreciation gratefully, with a sense of satisfaction, knowing she had worked hard for their approval. It had become more than just a desire to outshine Lizinka. Now, because of her growing commitment to the beautiful art of ballet, Sam wanted to be the best for her own sake.

She haunted the studio, coming to class early and lingering after the others had gone home. One late afternoon her mother called, worried, and Miss Jan laughingly told her that Sam was still there, safe and sound. Miss Jan understood Sam's love for dance, and would allow her to work quietly at the *barre* as long as she did not interfere with the practice of her regular classes.

Now and then Sam and Miss Jan would have little conversations about ballet, and Sam felt a bond with her teacher, who shared the same feelings about dance that she was beginning to develop.

The "Waltz of the Flowers" was a difficult but beautiful dance. Sam worked until she knew it perfectly. She even learned the Queen's part, and her toes became stronger as each day passed. She loved it all, but most of all she loved the dance that Lizinka, as Clara, did with the Prince. The dancer who took the part of the Prince was a handsome, blond boy about thirteen years old. Tom was tall, slim, and self-assured. When Lizinka came forward on her toes and extended her leg into an elegant *arabesque*, he would promenade around, turning her on the tip of her toe. It took Sam's breath away, it was so lovely. Then Lizinka would do two *piqué* turns and Tom would lift her high into the air, while her arms did a graceful *port de bras,* and her legs went into a *grand jeté*. Sam would watch as she continued to work quietly at the *barre*, determined that someday she would have her chance. When that time came, she would be prepared!

January, February, and March passed quickly by. Rehearsals began in earnest, and the girls started acting their parts. As one of the young guests, Samantha had to learn two German dances, which were lots of fun.

The march was done with the little "boy cousins," who were her own age. It was lively and gay; the boys teased, and the girls giggled, and that was the way Miss Jan liked it. It was a Christmas party, and they were supposed to be having fun.

The "Grandfather Dance" was done with the older teen-age boys, who took the parts of the uncles. It was a German folk dance, and the boys picked up the girls and whirled them right off their feet. They were breathless when they finished, cheeks rosy and eyes sparkling with laughter.

In the middle of the dance Uncle Drosselmeyer, who was very old and eccentric, wore a funny hat, and carried a crooked cane, pretended to be gruff and cross. The "cousins" had to make believe they were afraid of him.

Uncle Drosselmeyer came laden with gifts for the children. He gave Franz a drum, and Clara received a beautiful nutcracker made in the shape of a handsome soldier. This was the most exciting part of the ballet because Franz, who was jealous, grabbed it away from Clara and ran around and around, with the girls shrieking and the boys yelling. Franz's parents were so terribly embarrassed, they sent him to bed.

Samantha's part as a little cousin was over when the guests left, but she and the others all liked to watch Lizinka, as Clara, come back into the living room, cuddle in the big easy chair with her broken nutcracker, and pretend to fall asleep. Lizinka took it very seriously. When the Prince appeared from behind the Christmas tree and walked forward, arms outstretched to her, Samantha's friends all tittered and whispered. But Lizinka stayed in character. She solemnly reached her hand out and stood gracefully. The Prince then led her across the stage into the next scene, which was the Land of Snow.

When Lizinka and Tom did their *pas de deux*, Sam never left the studio until they had finished practicing. They worked terribly hard and never complained of being tired. It was then that Samantha realized why Miss Jan had chosen Lizinka. If Sam had not been exposed to Lizinka's hard work, she would never have realized how much is expected of a lead. Watching Lizinka work, she knew Miss Jan had been right in her choice. Another year—another time—Sam would be ready. She understood the demands now. At first she had thought only of the pretty costume and the glory of the part, never realizing that this glory must be earned through hard and dedicated work.

In April their costumes arrived. They were breath-taking in their beauty. Each was a different color—ballet-pink, sky-blue, sunshine-yellow, spring-green, pale orchid—all with classic *tutus* that stood straight out from the waist, making Sam aware of why they were taught to hold their arms rounded. It was to reach around the ballet skirts.

Samantha's costume was sky-blue and it was caught up with small clusters of pale pink roses. There was also a garland of pink rosebuds for her hair. She felt like a princess when she tried it on and put the flowers in her blond hair.

One day as they were rehearsing Act One, they came to the part where Uncle Drosselmeyer gave Clara the nutcracker, which made Franz jealous. He grabbed the nutcracker out of Clara's hands and ran around the living-room stage, followed by all the other little boy cousins. The girl cousins raced after them, and there was a tug of war; Franz and the boys pulled one way, and Clara and the girls pulled the other way until—kerplunk!—down went the girls and—crash!— the nutcracker landed on the floor and was broken. Clara burst into tears and ran to the dancer who was playing her mother.

Just at that moment the studio door opened, and a woman came in. She walked over to Miss Jan and said something to her in a low voice.

Miss Jan immediately went to the tape recorder and turned it off.

Lizinka looked up quickly, expecting a correction of some kind to be forthcoming since Miss Jan often stopped the music to offer suggestions or make changes of some kind.

"Lizinka," Miss Jan said with a smile, "your mother is here to pick you up. You may be excused for the rest of the day."

Lizinka's face flushed when she saw her mother. She immediately left the studio floor and went over to her. Putting her arm around her daughter's shoulder, Mrs. Petrovna said something to Lizinka that made her look sad.

Samantha couldn't help staring, concerned for her friend. Suddenly she became aware that everyone was looking at her.

"Put your toe shoes on," said Naomi. "Yes, go ahead."

"Hurry up," she heard her friends say.

Puzzled, she looked at Miss Jan.

"I don't think you heard me, Samantha. I asked you to take Lizinka's place for this rehearsal, please."

"Who, me?" stammered Samantha, feeling sure this was some sort of joke.

"Yes." Miss Jan laughed. "You. Will you hurry and

put on your toe shoes and warm up for the *pas de deux* with Tom?"

"I—I—I can't do that!" Samantha said desperately.

"Why, I thought you would jump at the chance. Don't you want to?" her teacher asked, puzzled.

"Oh, I do, I do, but, but, but—"

The class broke into laughter.

"You sound like a motorboat," said Michelle, giggling.

"The rest of you may leave now, and I'll work with Samantha and Tom alone for a while. See you all on Thursday," said Miss Jan.

As if in a dream, Samantha went over and started to put on her toe shoes. Her hands were cold, and her whole body felt numb. Could it really be true? Was she to practice the *pas de deux* with the Prince? Her fingers were so stiff, she fumbled as she tied the ribbons of her toe shoes. Automatically she walked over to the *barre* to warm up, as she had seen Lizinka do. Timidly she glanced over at Tom, who was preoccupied with a combination of steps he was trying to master.

"I'll never make it," Samantha said to herself. "They'll laugh at me." Frantically she continued working out until her body became more relaxed. She inhaled deeply, and her heart gradually stopped its wild pounding.

"I must keep calm. I must do my best," she reasoned sensibly to herself. "I *know* the dance. I've watched it enough. I've even practiced it, but always alone, never with a partner."

"Ready, Samantha?" Miss Jan asked, and she turned on the recorder. "Just do the best you can, dear. Tom will help you."

Shakily Samantha walked toward Tom. He reached out and took her hand. His hand was strong and steady. She stood on one toe and raised her leg into a high *arabesque.* Thank goodness I've been practicing at home, she thought. At least I can get my leg up above my waist. Not quite as high as Lee, but almost.

Slowly Tom started to promenade around with her. How strange it seemed, but fun. Suddenly when she was three quarters of the way around, she began to wobble on her toes. She lost her balance and down she went into a crumpled heap.

For a moment she thought she was going to cry. Then, looking up out of the corner of her eye, she could see Tom grinning down at her. She quickly glanced at Miss Jan, who was smiling, too. Why, they want to help me, she thought. They are not going to laugh at me 'cause I make mistakes. They're on my side, and I won't let them down. Jumping up quickly, she said in a quiet, steady voice, "I'm sorry. May I try that again? I think I can do it, with a little more practice."

"I'm sure you can, Samantha," said Miss Jan, and there was a look of pride on her face.

For over an hour they worked, quietly and steadily. Learning to hold their bodies erect and centered so as not to go off balance was not easy. But with repetition it became better, and by the end of the lesson it was a fairly presentable little *pas de deux*.

Miss Jan was pleased. Samantha could tell. And Tom seemed satisfied too.

"Lizinka's mother is going away for a month. She had to leave tonight. That is why she came for Lizinka," Miss Jan said. "There will be times when Lee won't be able to come to rehearsals, and I want Tom to continue his practice. On those occasions, Samantha," Miss Jan said seriously, "I'd like you to be Lizinka's understudy. That means when she is not here, I'd like you to practice in her place. Would you like that, Sam?"

"Would I? Wow! I'll say I would!" Samantha fairly shouted. Then, worried, she looked at Tom to see how he felt about it.

He was smiling and nodding his head. "Great," he said. "You make a fine understudy, and I do need the practice."

"I'll do my best," Samantha said solemnly, looking from one to the other, then quickly turned away as she felt the tears sting her eyes. What a day this has been, she thought. Do you suppose I'm dreaming?

"Mom! Mom!" shouted Samantha as she rushed into the kitchen. "Guess what?"

Samantha's brown eyes sparkled with joy. As usual, one blond braid on the top of her head had escaped the elastic band and was sticking straight out to one side, giving her a very impish look. Her flushed face was dead serious, however, and Mrs. Scott knew this was a matter that would demand her entire attention.

"What is it, Samantha?" she asked anxiously.

"I'm an understudy! I'm an understudy," shouted Sam joyously.

Mrs. Scott breathed a sigh of relief. Whatever it was all about, at least she could tell that it was good news.

"Simmer down!" She laughed. "What do you mean? Weren't you at ballet rehearsal today?"

"That's just it," Sam said eagerly. "I was at rehearsal, and Lizinka's mother came in to get her because she had to go away on a trip—her mother did, I mean—and Miss Jan asked me to take Lee's place."

Samantha stopped short, looking at her mother. Her brown eyes seemed to give off electric sparks. She had never been so excited.

"So you played the part of Clara in the first act?" her mother asked cautiously, still not quite sure.

"I mean, Mother," Samantha said, very slowly and distinctly, as if speaking to a small child who did not quite understand, "I mean, that I did the *pas de deux* with the Prince!"

"You did?" Mrs. Scott said, unbelieving. "Really?"

Before the words had escaped her lips, Samantha, who had been sitting tensely on the edge of the chair, could no longer contain herself. Like a tight coil unwinding, she sprang across the room, and before either of them knew what had happened, Sam was in her mother's arms, laughing and crying at the same time. All the tensions of the past two hours were released, and now she felt completely exhausted.

They were chattering like a couple of magpies and didn't notice Mr. Scott standing at the kitchen door.

Coming forward toward Samantha, he made a big awkward bow, saying, "Well, my little girl will be a famous ballerina yet!"

"Oh, Dad"—she giggled—"stop teasing. Who told you about it anyway?" she asked suspiciously.

"Why, I've been standing here for five minutes." Mr. Scott laughed. "Nobody noticed me, though. If this is what it's like to have a famous daughter, I'm not sure I'm going to like it."

"Oh, Dad, don't be silly. I'm only going to take Lee's place when she's not around, so Tom can keep up with his practice." She tried hard to be matter-of-fact about it all. But a grin played around her lips, and her sparkling eyes gave her away.

"Tell us about it, honey," Mrs. Scott insisted.

While Mrs. Scott made them some cocoa, Sam related in detail the events of the afternoon. She could even tell them about her tumble without feeling bad, knowing that she had made a lot of progress from that moment on.

"I think this calls for a celebration, don't you, Beth?" Mr. Scott said, looking over at his wife questioningly.

Pleased that he would realize the importance of the situation, Mrs. Scott smiled tenderly at her husband. The dinner she had started to prepare could be eaten tomorrow. This indeed was a special day for Sam. Remembering when her daughter had come home with a "stomachache," Mrs. Scott could smile now at how things had worked out. She was proud that Samantha had made the best of the situation and had gone on rehearsing harder than ever. Sam had learned a lot from that bitter lesson. Disappointments made success that much sweeter.

"Get your hats, ladies. I'm taking my two best girls out to dinner," Mr. Scott said gallantly.

"Hats?" they said, laughing. "What hats? Let's go!"

11

The Lady with the Silver Hair

It was customary for Miss Jan's classes to make a tour of the hospitals and nursing homes in the area. Some of the students danced, and others just paraded in their costumes. It was exciting; they met at the studio right after lunch and were excused from school, because the principal agreed it was a very worthwhile project. There would be about eight cars, filled with children in colorful costumes. Before they left on their tour, a local newspaper photographer would come and take their picture.

They would arrive at the hospital at an appointed

time, perform and model their costumes, and move on to the next place. The patients enjoyed it very much, and so did the children.

The class was doing the Kingdom of Sweets, which was the last act of *The Nutcracker*. This meant that Sam would be doing the "Waltz of the Flowers" with her class. Lizinka would be doing the *pas de deux* with the Prince. It would be the first time they had performed their dances before a live audience. Miss Jan told them they would never perform before a more appreciative gathering.

The hospital patients who were able would come down to the recreation rooms. They welcomed a change from the usual routine of the day. Miss Jan's students would start off with the costume parade, walking by the patients in a line and stopping a second if a patient expressed a desire to see the costume in detail. It was very informal and pleasant.

Thursday morning Sam woke up feeling a stir of excitement. Looking over, she could see her beautiful blue costume on the bureau, her toe shoes hanging by their ribbons from the mirror. Although she couldn't see them from her bed, she knew her pink tights were there, alongside the tiara of roses for her head. She knew she must get up soon and brush her hair an extra-long time today. It had to be bright and shiny for the performance.

"Samantha, dear," Mrs. Scott called up the stairs. "Time to get up. Breakfast is ready."

Almost before her mother had finished calling, Sam was out of her bed and into the bathroom. She splashed cold water on her face, brushed her teeth, and hurriedly put on her clothes. She gave her costume a little pat as she went past it and bounced down the stairs two at a time.

"Good morning, Sam," greeted her mother. "I thought perhaps you had decided not to go to school. It's such a dull schedule you have today." Her mother pretended to look very serious, but Sam could tell she was hiding a smile.

"Oh, Mom," Sam said, "I'm so nervous. I hope I don't forget my dance!"

"Well, if you do, so will everyone else," her mother replied. "No one could have practiced any more. I even hear the 'Waltz of the Flowers' in my sleep, you've played it so many times."

Samantha nibbled thoughtfully on a piece of crisp bacon, her brown eyes serious.

"Oh, I know it. It keeps going around and around in my brain. Only now I've added the *pas de deux*!"

"Oh, so that's the music I hear now more and more. It's lovely. But can you practice the *pas de deux* without a partner?" her mother asked.

"It isn't easy." Sam giggled. "I just pretend the bureau is the Prince and do my *arabesques* holding on to it. I pretend the knob on the middle of the mirror is his shoulder and the lower part of the mirror his wrist. That way I get used to the right positions."

Sam's nose wrinkled, and she gave a mischievous grin.

"What would Tom say if he knew his shoulder looked like a mirror knob?" teased her mother.

"He'll never know." Sam giggled. "I'll never tell!"

"I've been meaning to ask you why Lizinka can't be at rehearsals all the time. Did you ever find out? Nothing seriously wrong, I hope," her mother said.

"Oh no, not really. Lee said that the families of the delegates were being taken on special tours to historic landmarks like Gettysburg, Washington, D.C., and places like that. Since they'll be going back to Moscow right after the recital, her father thought they should take advantage of it. She really misses not being in class all the time, but" —Sam's eyes twinkled— "it's lucky for me!"

"I agree. They should see our country while they are here. It would be a shame not to," Sam's mother said. Then, glancing at the kitchen clock, she added, "Do you have all your things ready for this afternoon?"

"Yes, I do. I forgot to tell you I'll need money for supper. We're all going to stop off at Charlie's Place. Miss Jan thought it would be easier for parents since we'll be kind of late, and it will be fun for all of us."

"That's a good idea. What time do you think you'll be home?" asked her mother.

"At one-thirty we perform at Children's Hospital—that's the farthest away. Then we go to

Memorial at two-forty-five. At four o'clock we're due at Glenwood Home for the Aged. Our last performance is at five-thirty, and that's right in town; then on to Charlie's Place for supper."

"That's quite a schedule!" her mother said. "You'll be ready for bed when you get home, I'll bet. And," she said, looking at the clock, "you'll be late for school if you don't hurry."

Sam popped the last bite of toast into her mouth and jumped up from the table, almost knocking the chair over as she stood up.

As Sam ran down the path to meet her friends, her mother smiled to herself, thinking, How can she be so graceful on the ballet floor and so awkward around the house? Doesn't make sense.

The morning crept by at a snail's pace for Sam. Several of her dance friends were in her classroom, and they would sigh and roll their eyes heavenward as they caught each other sneaking looks at the big clock on the wall behind them. It seemed forever and a day before the bell rang for lunch, and even longer before it was time for them to meet outside the principal's office to be excused for the rest of the day.

When Sam arrived, the studio was in a hubbub. Squeals came from the dressing room as the girls changed into their costumes. Girls rushed from one end of the studio to the other, shouting to one another. There were five girls all trying to look into one mirror as they brushed their hair. Miss Jan was as excited as the rest of them, calling for them to change quickly because Mr. Brown, the photographer from the newspaper, would be arriving soon.

As Sam came out of the dressing room with her costume on, she saw Lizinka enter the studio already in her *pas de deux* costume. She looked simply beautiful! For a moment Sam felt a twinge of envy, but she quickly pushed the feeling aside. Right behind Lizinka came a man with a camera slung over his shoulder. Miss Jan started calling everyone to come and pose for a news picture.

After that they were given orders to stay with the same cars for the entire tour. Sam felt a hand slide into hers and looking over saw Lizinka smiling at her.

"Will you come with me, please?" Lizinka asked. "Boris is taking us. We can seat three more. Let's ask Lisa, Michelle, and Naomi to come, too."

So off they went to their first engagement. In the car they were rather quiet and nervous, deep in their own thoughts.

The first stop was Children's Hospital. The patients were already waiting in the recreation room when they arrived. Some children were in wheel-chairs; others had crutches by their chairs, arms in slings, heads bandaged, but all looked eagerly at the dancers as they entered, and Sam's heart skipped a beat. "We must do well for them," Samantha thought. "At least we are all well and strong."

The Lady with the Silver Hair

Standing in line waiting for the musical cue, Sam felt as if she had butterflies in her stomach, but as she heard the opening bars of the "Waltz of the Flowers," and the Queen of the Flowers moved gracefully across the floor on the tips of her toes, Sam forgot everything but her ballet steps. It was a joyous waltz, full of lively combinations, and the pastel *tutus* really did make them look like a flower garden.

Before she knew it, it was all over, and the smiling faces of the children expressed their joy and appreciation.

Swiftly Miss Jan urged them into their cars and on to the next place. All went well at Memorial Hospital, although they were a little cramped for space. Once again the faces of the patients expressed their thanks, and it was a happy and laughing group who got into the cars to head for the home for the aged.

Relaxed now, they chattered away, laughing over little episodes that had happened, but with a feeling of new self-assurance.

Arriving at the home, they were met by a nurse who escorted them into a large waiting room. The elderly people were gathering in the recreation room. Some were in wheelchairs; others had canes or were on the arms of nurses. In no time at all Miss Jan had the recorder on, and the strains of *The Nutcracker* came over the intercom. Glancing out the double door, Samantha spotted a small, silver-haired lady gently swaying and tapping her fingertips on the arm of her wheelchair. Sam was fascinated by the look on her face, by her obvious love of the ballet. She seemed entranced by the music, a faraway look in her eyes, completely oblivious to those around her.

The lady's friends nearby looked at one another with knowing nods and smiles, as though sharing a special secret. During Tom and Lizinka's *pas de deux*, she all but got out of her chair, so unmindful was she of everyone else. As the program came to an end and Sam turned to find Lizinka, she noticed that Miss Jan was taking her to meet the silver-haired lady. Curiosity got the best of her, so she lingered awhile and watched. She saw Lizinka nod as she listened earnestly to the little lady. Then she saw a very strange thing: Slipping back from the wheelchair, Lizinka swept into a beautiful *révérence*.

Still consumed with curiosity, Sam turned and walked quickly to the car, hoping she had not been discovered spying. Hearing light footsteps behind her, she turned to see Lizinka running toward her.

"She was a famous ballerina," Lizinka said. "She played the part of Clara when she was my age. She said I had talent—imagine me being complimented by a ballerina!" Lizinka's usually composed mouth smiled widely at Samantha.

Samantha understood Lizinka's joy, and she spontaneously put her arms about her friend and hugged her, realizing that they shared a common love of a demanding art. Then they ran to their waiting car.

The Lady with the Silver Hair

By the time they landed at Charlie's Place to eat, they were all merrily singing. Lizinka had even taught them a little Russian song. She sang the Russian words, and Sam, Michelle, Lisa, and Naomi accompanied her with the Russian equivalent of our "tra la la la." It went something like "vai do da do dee tallay," and they laughed at themselves until the tears streamed down their cheeks.

"Wow," said Michelle, "I never knew a foreign language was so much fun to learn!"

"Me either," Naomi agreed, popping a stick of gum into her mouth. "Join the club," Naomi said, grinning, as she passed Lizinka a stick of her precious gum.

"Oh, goom! Thank you very much!" Lizinka said, smiling back at Naomi. Lizinka didn't realize this was the mark of acceptance by Naomi.

"Can we have another lesson soon, Lizinka?"

"My pleasure," said Lizinka with much seriousness. Then, as an afterthought, a mischievous twinkle came to her eyes. "I've had, how you say it, a blast!"

They did indeed "have a blast." All of them. It had been a very successful and satisfying day.

12

Naked Rehearsal

It was a Saturday morning in May. They were to have
their first rehearsal on stage, at the Civic Center in
town. A naked rehearsal, it was called. All the class
had been taken aback for a moment when Miss Jan
had made this announcement. There had to be some
mistake. The children looked at one another. Naked
rehearsal! How could that possibly be? It took a
minute for Miss Jan to realize what was troubling her
dancers, their wide eyes looking back incredulously,
unbelievingly. Then the realization of what they
were thinking dawned on her. A hearty laugh burst

from her throat. The children, who had seen her many moods over the years, seldom saw this side of her: the almost girlish, uncontrollable laughter. Looking back at her, they joined in the merriment, a bit puzzled, but knowing perfectly well that Miss Jan would never expect them to dance in the nude!

"No, no, no, it's not what you're thinking," Miss Jan said, taking a deep breath and wiping away the tears that had trickled down her cheeks. "In the theater, a naked rehearsal means no sets and no costumes. We just get used to the stage and the surroundings. We find our places, and the backstage crew starts working on its part of the show. The lighting people begin aiming lights and setting in the color gels. The set designers begin arranging the sets on stage. The audio crew gets its equipment set up so that all is in readiness. There's a lot more to doing a ballet than learning dances.

"Although I must admit," Miss Jan added seriously, "the dancers are the most important of all, so we are depending on you to work very hard."

So much depends on us, Sam thought. I must not let a single day go by without rehearsing. She herself noticed how much stronger her body was now and how very much higher her elevation was this year. Why, she could get her leg up above her head and hold it there. Miss Jan even commented on how much she had improved.

Sam loved the rehearsals with Tom when Lizinka

had to be away. She became more self-assured. The melody of the *pas de deux* often went through her head on her way to school, in the study hall, before sleep at night. It seemed to haunt her. She found herself thinking more and more about her ballet. The more demanding it became, the better she liked it. If a particular step gave her trouble, she was more than ever determined to master it.

"That is the mark of a truly dedicated person," Miss Jan had said to her one day, after an especially difficult rehearsal. "To give up would be so much easier. That is what separates the many average ballet dancers from the few truly great ones. You have developed quality, Samantha, and if it continues as it has this year, you can lick the world."

Standing backstage in the wings with her class, all in their leotards and tights waiting for the introduction to the "Waltz of the Flowers," Sam felt the excitement. The girls were whispering, lights were being turned off and on to aim them, sets were being juggled around.

Before Sam had time to think of what to do in all this confusion, it was time to go on. Waltz two three, waltz two three, *piqué* turn, *piqué* turn. She stopped. Right beside a ladder!

Now what? she thought. Do I go in front of the ladder, behind it, or under it? she wondered. Standing there, looking up puzzledly at the man on the ladder, she realized the music had stopped and everyone was looking at her. A burst of laughter filled the stage.

"You looked so funny." Michelle chuckled.

"You acted like you thought you had to dance with the ladder," echoed Lisa with glee. Even Miss Jan joined in the fun.

"Come to the front of the ladder, Sam," she said with a smile. "Do the best you can, class. Just get used to the stage and the lights. It's good practice, and we have to work around each other since we only have use of the stage this morning."

And dance they did, around the ladder, around the lighting men, in and out among stage props, with blue lights turning to pink to amber and back to blue. "If we can dance through this," thought Samantha, "we can manage anything."

That evening she bubbled over while telling her mother and father about it. She even told them about the ladder, joining in the laughter as she told the story on herself. By the time supper was over and she was eating her dessert, a big yawn simply took over her body. "Ohhh," she sighed, stretching her arms high in the air.

"Well, well." Her father smiled across the table at her. "Someone will sleep well tonight, I'll bet."

And sure enough, Sam's head no sooner hit the pillow than she was asleep—no time even to review the day.

Finally it was time for dress rehearsal. Backstage was a beehive of activity. The dancers were lined up, being made up by backstage helpers. "Backstage angels," Miss Jan called them. They had to be angels, she said, to work so hard without any recognition. Without them there could be no show.

Each year a number of mothers would volunteer to help backstage. Samantha's mother was doing makeup this year, which meant she could go into the audience before the curtain went up and watch the entire performance. Sam was glad because she liked to know that her mother was out front watching her. She would watch the rehearsals and the matinee and evening performances, telling her father at supper how much better each performance became as the dancers got used to costumes, lights, and audience. After makeup they would gather in a large circle, all holding hands tightly, as Miss Jan gave them a little "pep talk," last-minute reminders, and words of encouragement to all. She would end by smiling and saying, "Well, class, break a leg." They would all break the circle, giggling nervously, for they knew that "break a leg" was a theater expression meaning "good luck." It was a way of supposedly dispelling the very thing that all people of the theater feared most: Breaking a leg meant no work, no perform-ance, no show. It was like throwing salt over your shoulder to ward off bad luck. Everyone knew it

was a silly custom; still everyone did it, just in case it might be true.

The overture was playing. The sets were all in place, houselights down, and work lights off. Act One was ready to begin.

At dress rehearsal the cast members who were not onstage were allowed in the audience to watch the performance, the only time they would see it in costumes with lights. It was thrilling, watching in the wings, waiting to go on. As the houselights dimmed and the curtain opened slowly, Samantha's heart skipped a beat. The audience was small, consisting only of dancers, backstage angels, and lighting and backstage crew, all quietly watching the production they had helped to create. Each had his or her job, and each watched for flaws and last chances to improve on his or her work, whatever it might be.

There was no stopping the music this time. Good, bad, or otherwise, the tape rolled along. Whatever mistakes were made Miss Jan corrected over the sound, and on went the performance.

The Christmas Party with Clara, Franz, the little cousins, and the aunts and uncles was a little stiff. Everyone was doing his or her part correctly, but without the spontaneity that Miss Jan kept trying to bring out at rehearsals. Sam's smile felt frozen as she entered and was greeted by the Governor and his wife. It felt stiff and unreal. Looking at the others, she sensed they were all having the same problem.

Gradually, though, as the scene progressed, she began to relax and enjoy the party, just as she would have had it been real. They had "punch" and cookies, and the coolness of the punch went down her throat, soothing it and cooling her parched lips. By the time they had to run after Franz, who had grabbed the nutcracker from Clara, they had begun to relax.

"Good, good, keep it up," Miss Jan said over the music. "It's a wonderful party, and you're having fun, remember."

Much too soon for Samantha, the scene was over, and she was putting on her velvet cloak and saying good-bye with a curtsy to the Governor and his wife. With a last wave in the wings, off they went.

Once offstage, they dropped their characters as they shed their velvet cloaks and started to giggle and talk, forgetting momentarily that there was still action on stage and they had to be quiet. A backstage mother firmly shushed them, reminding them that every sound could be heard out front.

Standing in the darkness backstage, Samantha imagined Lizinka going through her part. This was special, and Sam had watched it dozens of times at rehearsals. She had even done it a number of times when Lizinka was away, and now in her mind's eye, with the music as her cues, she stood still and went through the motions she knew Lizinka was making on stage.

A flurry in the wings told her that Clara had come off stage. Then, with the help of her backstage mother, she had donned her nightgown and tiptoed back to the Christmas tree by the little crib that held the bandaged nutcracker. She sat in the big easy chair, cuddling the toy while she dreamed of the Prince who would suddenly come alive and take her hand, leading her into the Land of Snow.

Samantha ached to be out there, taking the part of Clara. But her day would come, she felt sure, especially if she continued to work hard. She had not missed the approving glances of Miss Jan as she had rehearsed with the *corps de ballet* and also the few times she had taken Lizinka's place. Her teacher was not given to undue praise, but when it was deserved she would comment with great sincerity. A bond had grown between teacher and student. My day will come, Samantha thought again. Wait and see!

Then suddenly Samantha was brought abruptly back from her "star dreams" as the curtain closed on Act One and the cast burst into the dressing room, almost picking her up in the exodus. Time for the change for the Kingdom of Sweets. There were about ten minutes, and if they hurried, they could go out in front and watch the Snow Queen and the Snowflakes, which Sam had never seen in costume under the lights.

Excitedly Samantha pulled on her beautiful blue costume, placing the crown of rosebuds on her head.

Pushing her feet into the toe shoes, she wriggled her toes into place. A few *pliés* and she'd be ready. Standing off in a corner, she started to bend and stretch. Some of the other girls followed suit. They had been taught to warm up their muscles before dancing so as not to injure themselves and in order to dance their best. They heard the introduction to the Snow Queen's dance, and rather than exercise they all dashed up the corridor to the auditorium, some still not completely dressed, but all eager to watch the only other *corps de ballet,* this one made up of the older, more advanced girls.

As they stepped into the auditorium, Samantha caught her breath. The stage was transformed into a forest of fir trees, covered with snow. The ballerinas were all dressed in short, white *tutus* with silver sparkling touches, and the Snow Queen wore a long, white romantic *tutu* with a silver crown on her head. As the dancers whirled and twirled in the blue light, a soft flurry of snow began to fall. This had to be the most beautiful sight she had ever seen!

"Hurry, hurry, girls," Samantha heard the voice of a backstage mother whisper. "The Kingdom of Sweets is next."

Rushing up the corridor to the stage, Samantha thought she heard someone gasp, but she was in too much of a hurry to stop and look back. As she waited for her cue, while the stage crew flew around changing sets, yanking off the fir trees and setting up the throne which would hold Clara, she saw an excited group of girls all desperately trying to fix something. Moving closer, she could see that a backstage mother was threading a needle, and there was Naomi, eyes full of tears, with her pale-yellow net skirt pulled right away from the bodice, hanging to the floor.

"I can't go on like this," she sobbed.

"All right, all right, just quiet down," the backstage mother reassured her. "Lucky I brought a needle and thread."

With fingers flying, she deftly sewed the net back up to the satin bodice as the introduction to the "Waltz of the Flowers" reached their ears.

"I can't go on," cried Naomi.

"Places, everyone," Miss Jan called softly, firmly pushing everyone into line.

"What will I do, oh, what will I do?" sobbed Naomi.

"You will go on, that's what you'll do," Miss Jan said firmly as the last stitch went into place, needle still dangling from the *tutu*.

"Now think, girls. Waltz two three, waltz two three, *piqué* turn, *piqué* turn. Think, girls, smile, girls, you're on," and poor Naomi, quickly wiping the tears from her eyes, had no choice but to go on. But before she reached the center of the stage, a smile had touched her lips and her dimples dug deep into her cheeks.

That night, as Sam was telling her parents about it, able now to laugh at what had seemed a tragedy at the time, her father asked the very logical question that Sam had not even thought to ask: "How did Naomi tear her costume?"

Puzzled, Samantha said, "Why, I don't know. We didn't think to ask." Then, with a twinkle in her eye, she said, "You know, Dad, the show must go on!"

13

Curtain Calls and Red Roses

The day of the matinee was bright and clear. A soft breeze was blowing, billowing the curtains of Sam's bedroom window. Stretching her body with a luxurious yawn, Sam lay there, thinking about the matinee that afternoon. This was what they had been working toward all year, and now the day had come at long last.

Remembering the excitement of the dress rehearsal, Samantha's heart skipped a beat. "Please let everything go well today," she whispered softly to herself. This was the real thing! Last night she had been so excited and tired, she had popped into bed without getting her things ready. So today she had to rinse out her tights, press her costume, and fix her hair. It had to be shampooed, dried, then brushed and pulled up in a topknot so the halo of flowers could encircle it.

Going downstairs, she wondered why her mother hadn't called. It must be almost eight o'clock. She would have to hurry to get to school on time. Looking at the hall clock, she stopped short and blinked her eyes. It must be wrong. The clock must have stopped last night. But the pendulum was swinging, and it said eleven-thirty!

"Mom, Mom," she called, "what time is it? Am I late for school?"

"Here I am," her mother called from the patio.

Sam burst through the screen door and almost knocked over a chair in her haste.

"Calm down, dear." Her mother smiled reassuringly. "I called the school, and they said you needn't come in. All the girls are excused. It's just 'cleanup day,' and you can do your desk on Monday. So I let you sleep. I think you needed it, because I've looked in on you three times and you were sleeping very soundly."

"Oh, wow!" Sam said, "I can't believe it. I guess I was really tired."

Then once again she rubbed her eyes. There, gently swaying on the line, as though dancing a graceful waltz, was her blue costume and beside it her pink tights. Her Mom even had her toe shoes airing out.

"Oh, Mom." Sam smiled. "You got my things ready—thanks a million." And she planted a kiss on her mother's cheek.

"Sit down, honey, and have a bowl of cereal. After you eat, you can shower and shampoo your hair."

Samantha stifled a yawn and sat at the picnic table. She poured the cereal into a bowl, added cream, and started to eat, gazing out on the line, watching her costume turn gently to and fro. She started to hum the "Waltz of the Flowers." Her mother smiled to herself and thought, It will be strange when this is all over tomorrow night: no more frantic rehearsals, no more lessons until next fall, and soon school will be over. Whatever will Sam do with her time?

Shampoo over, hair dried, costume packed, the time suddenly seemed to fly by, and it was one o'clock. Time to go. Her father was unable to be at the whole matinee but had promised to drop in for the last act to see Sam and her class do the "Waltz of the Flowers."

Arriving at the civic center with her mother, Sam entered the building and went to the backstage dressing room as instructed. Some of the performers were already there, being made up. Sam went directly to the private dressing room assigned to the "Waltz of the Flowers" girls.

Michelle, Lisa, Karen, Debby, Evie, Sheri, Beth, Paula, Naomi, and Lizinka were all there, most of them in their costumes. A hush had fallen over the cast, quite different from the hubbub of the dress rehearsal. Occasionally someone would giggle, but it was quickly stifled, almost as if they knew that if they allowed their emotions to get out of hand, they would really fall apart into a state of nerves.

Sam quickly got into her party dress for Act One. The others soon left to line up for makeup.

"Act One cast in line first," the makeup mothers kept saying, echoed by Miss Jan, who was flitting from one group to another, counting noses to see that all had arrived.

The boys in Act One were grimacing over the fact that they had to wear makeup. Some of the girls were complaining about how strange it felt, too. By the time the last character in Act One was ready, the music of the beautiful overture was reaching their ears.

"Ten minutes to curtain time," shouted Paul, the stage manager, from the stage door.

An excited hum like the buzzing of bees filled the backstage. Sam could feel the tensions mounting. She found herself standing next to Lizinka, and a warm feeling of love swept over her. She had forgotten until that moment that after tomorrow night Lizinka would be going back to Moscow. She had been so busy and involved with the present, she hadn't thought beyond that time. How strange it would be not to have her in class next year! "I've learned so much from her about discipline and hard work," thought Sam. It was almost as though Lizinka could feel Sam's thought waves because they both reached out their hands to each other and squeezed hard.

"Good luck, Lee," Sam said, smiling.

"Break a leg, Sam," Lizinka said softly, with an impish grin which would have been out of character for her just a few months before. Lizinka, too, had learned from Samantha: She could now relax and enjoy ballet for the pure love of it.

"Two minutes before curtain," Paul called.

"Places, everyone," Miss Jan called. "This is it, dancers! Do your very best, everyone!"

With that, there was a rush to line up in the wings. "Watch the cables underfoot," Doug, the backstage man, whispered over and over.

Backstage mothers were shushing everyone.

"Quiet, quiet, quiet, dancers, and careful underfoot," they said softly as the Act One cast went into the darkened backstage.

The Governor, his wife, Clara, and Franz, with a wave of their hands to those left behind, went onto the living-room set and got into character just as the curtain began to rise.

"They just made it!" whispered Michelle.

"Wow!" breathed Lisa. "Just in time."

They didn't realize that this was the way Miss Jan had planned it. She knew that standing around waiting for curtain time would make them nervous.

Sam was third in line to go onstage with her "parents." She hardly had time to rearrange her blue velvet cloak and adjust her white fur hat when she found herself being gently pushed onstage. A tight little smile that felt stiff and strange touched her face.

Mechanically she removed her cloak and hat and handed them to the maid. Walking primly over to the Governor and his wife with her "parents," her legs felt like two sticks. She curtsied stiffly, as she was expected to do; then, receiving a pat on the head from te Governor, she was urged by her "mother" to run and play with the other young guests.

The children were beside the Christmas tree, looking at packages and talking to one another, trying to appear as casual and natural as they could. Suddenly Sam heaved a big sigh. It was so loud that the young guests, startled, looked over at her.

"Why, this is fun!" Sam thought. "I love being onstage and pretending." She smiled a mischievous smile and gave Naomi a little push with her shoulder. "You're at a party, remember," she mimicked Miss Jan. Those hearing her whisper couldn't help but smile. Miss Jan, observing from the wings, nodded appreciatively.

"Good, good, they're really into it now," Miss Jan whispered.

Mrs. Scott and the other makeup women nodded and smiled at one another. "Why, those children look like they are really at a Christmas party—they're doing fine." And settling back into their seats they, too, began to enjoy themselves.

Act One went beautifully. Everyone was "putting out" one hundred percent, and Lizinka as Clara had never done better. During the scene when they had to pretend to eat their refreshments, Sam suddenly thought of something. Going over to Lizinka, she whispered, "Are your folks here today?"

"Yes, oh yes," Lizinka answered, eyes sparkling with joy. "They both could make it."

Smiling happily, Samantha moved on to her next cue, thinking how wonderful it was that Lee's parents could be there to see her perform.

Act One was almost finished, and the cast waited in the wings, being careful not to make any unnecessary noise. The soft music played on, while backstage a frantic scene took place. Three backstage mothers, each with a job to do, helped whip off Clara's party dress, put on her nightgown, and tie back her dark-brown hair so it hung down her back in soft curls.

Taking a deep breath, Lizinka stepped out onto the stage to take her nutcracker soldier from under the Christmas tree and curl up in the big easy chair.

Samantha closed her eyes and envisioned Clara when the Prince appears and takes her to the Land of

Snow. So completely did she imagine each move that when the curtain was down, she was almost knocked over when the cast all moved back toward the wings at once.

Back in the dressing room, the girls chattered a mile a minute. They had plenty of time to get into their "Waltz of the Flowers" costumes, but Sam wanted to be able to watch Lizinka and Tom in their *pas de deux*. She knew that if she was ready when Lizinka was, she could slip into the wings unnoticed by anyone.

By the time the backstage crew had set up the fir trees for the Land of Snow, they were ready. Twelve teens waiting in their lovely white-and-silver costumes and the Snow Queen in her romantic white-and-silver *tutu* — all were warming up before going on. Clara looked lovely in her pink-and-silver *tutu*, and the Prince in his cavalier costume looked absolutely elegant.

Samantha looked over and caught Tom's and Lizinka's eyes. Tom winked, and Lizinka smiled and crossed her fingers. Sam felt a rush of tears. "They know I understand. We've all worked together and developed a special bond," she thought.

As Tom and Lizinka danced their *pas de deux* onstage in the semidarkness, Miss Jan, pretending not to see, smiled to herself as she watched Sam's lithe body go through all the steps possible without a real partner. She knew that next year, if the part was right, Sam would be ready for a lead. She would not forget how Sam had worked this year, and she took a special pride in Samantha's work.

Samantha slipped back into the dressing room. In all the excitement she hadn't even been missed! The girls were warming up in their toe shoes, looking for all the world like a colorful garden of flowers in their pastel *tutus*.

"Ready, girls!" Miss Jan called. "Kingdom of Sweets next."

How fast it all seemed to go! At rehearsal there was so much starting and stopping that the acts seemed long, but now it all flew by.

Rushing backstage, trying to be quiet as they lined up but feeling the stir of excitement, they knew this was the real thing.

"Watch the cables, girls," Doug, the stagehand, reminded them once again.

Then came the introduction of their beautiful "Waltz of the Flowers." Her father was watching, Sam knew. She must really do her best. As if in a dream, she heard Miss Jan softly whisper, "Smile, girls! Think, girls! Waltz two three, Waltz two three."

It was heavenly. Once onstage, Samantha and all the girls danced their hearts out.

"The season's hard work has all been worth it," Miss Jan said, smiling approvingly at her eleven young toe dancers, remembering their moans and groans and those first lessons *en pointe*!

Then it was over.

All except curtain calls, the most fun of all!

As each group came forward to make their bow—their *grande révérence*—the audience applauded enthusiastically. Samantha tried to find her father and mother as she made her *grande révérence* with the "Waltz of the Flowers" girls, but all she could see was a blur of faces.

Last came the leads, Clara and the Prince—Lizinka and Tom.

Samantha's heart swelled with pride for her two friends. Red roses for Lizinka were presented to her by her Cavalier, Tom.

Applause—applause—applause!

Music to their ears! What an appreciative audience!

How elegantly Lizinka took her bows—like a real ballerina, Sam thought.

At last the curtain closed, and laughingly they all rushed offstage at once, stumbling over one another in their haste. Samantha was trying hard to reach the wings because her father had said he would be waiting there for her. Suddenly a cry of pain reached her ears. Everyone seemed to freeze.

"She tripped on the cable," they whispered to one another, eyes wide in disbelief.

"Who is it?" Sam asked someone.

"All right, dancers' —Miss Jan's voice came to their ears— "please move along! It's all right. You've done a beautiful job. See you all tomorrow."

And the backstage mothers gently eased them all out, but not before Samantha saw that the ballerina on the floor holding her ankle, red roses spread around her, was Lizinka!

14

An Urgent Call

Driving home with her parents, Samantha couldn't get out of her mind the picture of Lizinka holding her ankle in pain.

"She'll be all right, Sam," her mother said. "Please stop worrying. You're all very tired, and after a nice bath and supper, I'm sure she'll be good as new. We'll phone her house when we get home."

"I was proud of you, Samantha," her father said. "Were there other girls dancing with you or was that a solo? You were the only one I saw on that stage."

"Oh, Dad. You do say such nice things."

An Urgent Call

Forgetting about Lizinka for a while, Sam overflowed with excitement, talking about all the incidents backstage and onstage, and ending with a wistful "It was such fun!"

Mrs. Scott, knowing the family would all be coming home weary, had planned a light casserole supper with salad, sherbet, and iced lemonade. By the time it was over, Samantha was almost ready for bed, so drained was she from the performance.

"Will you call Lizinka's house now, Mom?" Sam asked worriedly.

"I will, but first take a nice hot bath and get into your nightgown. I'll phone while you're doing that."

It was lucky Samantha was not watching her mother's face when she talked to Mrs. Petrovna. A worried frown crossed her brow, and she shook her head from side to side, saying, "Oh, what a shame. I hope so, yes, elevate it, and cold packs. These things can be painful, I know. I hope by morning things will look better. Good-bye, Mrs. Petrovna."

Wiping the worried look from her face, Mrs. Scott went upstairs to Sam's room.

Looking searchingly at her mother, Sam said, "How is she?"

"Not too bad. She's as tired as you are, and the pain is gone. They are hopeful by morning she'll be good as new."

"I hope so," Sam said sleepily. "We couldn't have our *Nutcracker* ballet without Clara!"

"Oh, I'm sure she'll be fine by then," her mother said, tucking Samantha in and kissing her on the top of her head. "Go to sleep, dear. You've had a busy day, and I am so proud of you."

"Mmmmm," Sam murmured, and almost before her mother had closed her door, she was sound asleep.

Early the next morning the phone rang, startling Mrs. Scott so that she almost spilled her coffee at the breakfast table.

"Who could be calling so early?" she said as she hurried to answer it.

"Good morning, Miss Jan," Mrs. Scott said into the phone. "Good morning. I should think you would be sleeping late this morning after such a busy and successful matinee."

Then, as she listened, a startled expression came over her face.

"Oh no. Oh dear. I don't know. I know she has been practicing, but she never expected to perform. Oh, Miss Jan, yes, just give me a minute to get used to the idea. All right, I'll call you back as soon as I've talked with Samantha."

Placing the receiver back on the cradle, she gazed off into space for a while, a concerned look on her face.

Tapping lightly on Samantha's bedroom door, Mrs. Scott went in and looked tenderly down at her daughter. "Hope she's well rested," she thought.

"She's about to start the most eventful day of her life."

As she looked, Sam's brown eyes opened, and seeing her mother standing over her, she sat up quickly.

"Am I late, Mom?" she asked. "What time is it?"

"It's early. Stop worrying." And sitting on the edge of her bed, Mrs. Scott took a deep breath and tried to imagine how her daughter would take the news she was about to tell her. There was so much to be done today, they really couldn't waste a minute.

"Samantha," Mrs. Scott said, taking Sam's hand in hers, "Miss Jan just called. . . ."

A puzzled look came over Sam's face, but she waited for her mother to go on.

"You see, Samantha, Lizinka's ankle is not better. . . ." She paused a second, letting her statement sink in.

Samantha's expression changed to one of concern.

"Oh, it's not serious, dear," her mother assured her quickly, realizing her daughter's fears. "It's just that she won't be able to dance tonight."

There, the words were out! Mrs. Scott took a deep breath, and this time she waited for her daughter to speak.

"Not dance tonight?" Samantha's eyes looked like two huge saucers. "Not dance tonight!" she repeated. "How will we do *The Nutcracker*?"

"Well," Mrs. Scott said, trying to be calm, "Miss

Jan says you must get ready to do her part, since you are her understudy."

"Me!" Sam's voice exploded. "Me!" she said again in disbelief. "I can't do that!"

"Miss Jan thinks you can, Samantha," Mrs. Scott said firmly, realizing that she had to convince Sam that it was an obligation she had to fulfill, and soon.

"Get into your practice clothes and come down to breakfast. Miss Jan is already at the studio. There are costumes to fit and alter, and Tom will be there soon to rehearse, so better get a move on."

In five minutes, Sam was downstairs in her leotard and tights, a baffled but determined look on her face. Too excited to eat much, she drank the orange juice her mother offered her, ate half a piece of toast, and was ready to go.

Arriving at the studio with her mother, she found Miss Jan there with Mrs. Petrovna, who was holding the red velvet dress that Lizinka wore in Act One. Miss Jan was holding the beautiful pink-and-silver *pas de deux* costume. It was at this point that Sam really realized that she was going to be taking Lizinka's place. The thought was overwhelming!

Samantha's eyes searched Miss Jan's face. What she saw there made her heart turn over. Miss Jan was worried too.

A quick little sob escaped her throat, and the next thing she knew, she was in Miss Jan's arms. She couldn't tell if the pounding she felt was Miss Jan's heart or her own. It just felt comforting.

"There, there, honey," Miss Jan said softly, patting her shoulders. "There, there."

Then, cupping Samantha's face with her two hands and looking deep into Samantha's eyes, she said, "I know you can do it, Samantha. I know you'll come through for me."

Samantha's chin trembled, but her lips broke into a tremulous smile.

"I won't let you down, Miss Jan. I promise!"

"Ahem, hum, hum, where do I fit in this picture?" The teasing voice of Tom met their ears.

"Oh, Tom, you're here," Miss Jan said, and with a quick squeeze of Sam's shoulders, she said, "Let's get down to business. We have a lot of work to do."

And work they did! First the costumes were tried on, so they could be altered. Fortunately Sam and Lizinka were very close in size, with Sam just slightly shorter.

They went over the first act several times. It didn't give Sam any real trouble, except that when she heard her own cue as the young guest, she felt strange not responding to it. Samantha had been onstage the entire act, so she found it quite easy to take over Clara's part, and fun too. Miss Jan had called the young guests for a quick run-through. She had decided it would not be necessary to use anyone in Sam's place. Better not confuse the issue any more. Everyone pitched in and helped. They all wanted to see this through together.

They talked over the quick change from party dress to nightgown and decided to use the same backstage mothers and not involve Mrs. Scott. In fact, they decided it was best all around for Mrs. Scott not to be backstage at all except for her regular makeup job.

"I'd probably make Sam more uptight," she said, laughing nervously. She was finding it harder than Sam to get used to the idea. Besides, Samantha was so busy rehearsing, she had hardly had time to think.

"Guess I'll go home and hem up this party dress and adjust the other costume. Then I'll get a light supper ready for Sam."

"Just give her some broth, Mrs. Scott. She'll perform better with less to eat. Plan on her eating after it's over," said Miss Jan.

"I'm sure you're right, Miss Jan, but won't she be hungry?"

"Oh, we'll send out for food at noon for all of us. She'll be hungry enough then to eat after the workout she'll be getting. Eating with Tom and me will help her to really feel we're a team. Then I'll send her home to rest awhile. I'll need her at the auditorium by six to practice some more onstage. It's hectic, I know, Mrs. Scott, but I think she'll gain a lot from this experience."

"Guess we all will." Mrs. Scott laughed. "I know

I'll never be the same." And gathering the costumes in her arms and waving to Sam and Tom, she left.

They must have done the *pas de deux* a dozen times. It reached the point where it felt natural and familiar.

It was an adjustment for Tom, too. Even the slight difference in Sam's weight and height changed the balance point so that he had to promenade at a different pace.

"That was just lovely, Tom and Samantha," Miss Jan said. "I'll be so happy if you do that well tonight."

"Oh, we will, won't we, partner?" Tom said, grinning at Sam. He was really trying his best to make Sam feel at ease.

They sent out for hamburgers and Cokes, and after running through some of the trouble spots, Miss Jan decided they had worked long enough.

"See you at six onstage," she said as she let Sam off at home. "Better get some rest."

Dropping wearily into the kitchen chair, Sam repeated what Miss Jan had said.

"Imagine her thinking I could sleep today."

"Well, at least get out of your practice clothes and lie down and read," her mother suggested.

Ten minutes later, she decided to look in on her daughter. There, stretched out on the bed in dungarees and shirt, ballet book on chest, lay Samantha, fast asleep!

15

The Big Night

The gentle strains of *The Nutcracker*'s overture filled
the auditorium as the ushers led the patrons to their
seats. A special stir of interest could be felt when Mr.
and Mrs. Petrovna, Nanatasha, and Lizinka on
crutches came down the aisle and seated themselves
in the places reserved for them by Miss Jan. Quickly
following them down the aisle came Mr. Scott, who
sat down next to them with a nod and a smile. The
seat next to him was conspicuously empty, as it was
reserved for Mrs. Scott, who was still doing makeup
backstage. The rustling of programs, the settling of

people in their seats, the leaning over to speak to the person in front of or beside them, created an atmosphere of expectancy. Word had quickly spread through Brighton of Lizinka's accident at the matinee, so it was with great curiosity that the audience waited for the curtain to rise.

Backstage, Samantha and Tom had been rehearsing for almost two hours. The cast had arrived, and a very deep undercurrent could be felt: the knowledge that each one would have to do his or her best to help make this evening a success.

Lizinka had phoned Samantha late in the afternoon and wished her luck. Sam had complimented her on her performance at the matinee, and Lizinka had wistfully commented on how happy she was that her parents had been there to see her. Naturally Lizinka was disappointed but was being a very good sport about it all.

"I'll be in the front row tonight with my family," she told Sam, "and I'll keep my fingers crossed for you until the curtain falls."

The stage lights flicked their warning. Houselights came down slowly. The final bars of the overture reached their ears, and up went the curtain.

For a wild moment, Samantha felt like fleeing. Her heart beat against her ribs like a wild bird trapped in a cage. The sea of faces looking up at her seemed very unfriendly. Suddenly her eyes focused on the front row, and she knew she was not alone; everyone there was rooting for her. She knew it as surely as if they had all stood up and cheered.

Once Samantha became accustomed to pretending to be Clara, she threw herself into the part with great gusto. Because she was an outgoing girl by nature, her portrayal was more flamboyant than Lizinka's, and while each was good in its own way, Samantha's had a touch of comedy. The audience responded with chuckles as she ran after her brother when he snatched the nutcracker from her. Back and forth they went in the tug-of-war between boy cousins and girl cousins, and Samantha in her enthusiasm pulled harder than necessary and landed on the floor with a thud. Her eyes opened wide—the pain was real, and she responded with a glare that brought down the house. From that moment on Clara had the audience in the palm of her hand, and she loved it.

Mr. and Mrs. Scott looked at one another and smiled. They could relax now. Samantha was in full control.

After the hectic change into her nightgown, Samantha walked onto the stage lit only by the Christmas-tree lights. Taking the nutcracker from under the tree, she sank into the deep cushioned armchair and pretended to sleep.

Then, right on cue, as if by magic, there was Tom, her Cavalier, her Prince, reaching his hand out to her. Mimicking Lizinka, she stretched her hand out with all the dignity and poise she could summon and followed as he led her to the Land of Snow.

As the curtain came down on Act One, Samantha breathed a sigh of relief and collapsed into the nearest chair backstage. The young guests gathered round her, chattering noisily.

"Did you hurt yourself when you landed on your behind?" asked Naomi, with a twinkle in her eye.

"Oh, did I!" Samantha said, rolling her eyes heavenward.

"I thought it was fun," Evie said. "Like a real tug-of-war."

"Guess I did forget for a second where I was." Samantha laughed.

"Yeah, and that's when I let go," Tony said gleefully, rubbing his hands together. He had enjoyed his part as Franz.

"All right, dancers, better get ready for the next act," Miss Jan said, and looking at Samantha, she nodded her head approvingly. "Keep it up, Sam! You're doing just fine."

Slipping into the pink-and-silver costume, Samantha glanced at herself in the full-length dressing-room mirror. She had been so busy all day that she had not even had time to see herself in it. Her mother and Miss Jan had decided what needed altering, and that was the last she had thought of it until now. She had loved her blue "Waltz of the Flowers" *tutu*, but this *pas de deux* costume was so elegant it took her breath away. Her hair was up on the top of her head, with tiny little tendrils escaping at the nape of her neck; her eyes were starry with excitement; and her cheeks were several shades pinker than her costume.

If only I can get through this *pas de deux*, so I won't disappoint Miss Jan, she thought. Guess I'd better warm up my muscles. I have about five minutes.

She went down slowly and up slowly in *grands pliés*, then *tendus*, then *grands battements* and *ports de bras*, bending and stretching and stretching and bending until she could feel her body grow warm and supple. She was used to slipping out with Lizinka at this point, so she could watch unobserved backstage. Now she was going out there in front of an audience by herself!

As she entered the backstage area, she could see Tom and the teens in their Snowflake costumes, warming up. And there, standing in the wings, leaning on her crutches, was Lizinka—a big smile on her face.

"I couldn't sit still, not for this part," Lizinka said. "You were really good in Act One."

"Oh, Lee, I'm so scared. I can't dance like you. I'm not nearly as good as you are," Sam said earnestly.

"Nonsense," Lizinka said. "A ballerina must be ready to step in at a moment's notice."

And Samantha, looking at her, knew that had the roles been reversed, Lizinka would have come through with flying colors.

The Big Night

Lizinka had taught her so much. In spite of the keen disappointment she must be feeling at not being able to perform on this night of nights, she was helping Samantha overcome her fear.

How could I ever have thought she was like an icicle? Sam wondered. Why, she's one of my best friends!

"Act Two ready," called the stage manager.

"Places, everyone," Miss Jan called. First the Snow Queen danced, followed by her Snowflake *corps de ballet*. Looking at the blue stage with the snowflakes gently falling, Sam couldn't believe she was actually going out there to dance. It was breathtaking in its splendor. But here she was entering on the tips of her toes, with the Prince walking beside her. As she waved her hand, the Snowflakes bowed down, leaving a pathway for Clara and the Prince to follow.

Thank goodness I practiced, thought Samantha, her eyes shining.

Light as feathers, they moved from one *divertissement* to another. Tom's firm grasp reassured her that she was doing fine. A faint smile touched her lips as she stretched her leg into an *arabesque pencheé*, higher and higher and higher, until she knew it was her very best effort.

In the wings Miss Jan and Lizinka exchanged glances. Sam's extension was not as high as Lizinka's, but what she lacked in technique, she added in warmth and sincerity.

"I love it, I love it, I love it!" Samantha seemed to say to Tchaikovsky's haunting *pas de deux*.

And the audience watching her knew it.

All too soon for Samantha, it was over. All too soon, it was time for the curtain calls, the applause, and, finally, as the star, her turn to bow.

"Try to be like Lizinka," Sam said to herself. "Be elegant. Act like a princess."

But as she swept into her *grande révérence* to the audience, she glanced at her father in the front row, and with a mischievous grin she gave him a great big wink.

The audience roared.

Tom came on with her roses. But before he could present them to her, Sam ran into the wings, and taking Miss Jan with one hand and Lizinka with the other, she pulled them onstage with her.

As if on signal, the audience cheered.

Tears streaming down their cheeks, but with smiles on their faces, Lizinka and Sam hugged each other.

Backstage in the wings, craning their necks and standing on tiptoe to see better, Samantha's class gave a "Bravo! Bravo, Sam and Lee!"

As the curtain came down for the last time. Samantha swept into a *grande révérence* to Lizinka—a *révérence* that she knew her friend would understand.

The cast cheered and applauded, and the audience

stood, giving a standing ovation to Sam, Lizinka, and Miss Jan.

Lizinka, as best she could on her crutches, returned the respectful bow to her American friend—then she grinned at Sam.

The lives of the two young dancers from different parts of the world would never be the same. They would both always remember what they had learned together—and from each other—the year they went *en pointe* and shared the lead role in Miss Jan's recital.